THE ONES LEFT BEHIND

ELIZABETH JOHNS

UNTITLED

Brethren in Arms

PROLOGUE

Vitoria, Spain, June 1813
The Allied Encampment

*T*he grief was so thick in their throats none could speak. They had been together for only two years, yet the bonds of the battle were forged stronger than any created by blood. It was not something that could be explained, only experienced.

When they had set sail from England for the Peninsula, each had felt invincible, ready to conquer evil and save England. Now, it was hard to remember why they needed to be brave anymore.

James shivered. There was a chill in the air as they all sat huddled around the fire. The silence the night before a battle was eerie, but after, it was deafening. Watching the flames perform their blue, gold and orange dance, it did not seem real that one of them was gone. They had survived Ciudad Rodrigo, Badajoz, and Salamanca, yet Peter had fallen before their eyes today. His sabre had been raised and his eyes fierce, ready to charge when a shot had seared through him. He was on his horse one moment and gone the next. The scene replayed over and over in their minds in slow-motion. Memory was a cruel, cruel master. The same battle had left Luke wounded when a shell exploded near him. He insisted on joining them, eschewing the orders of the sawbones and hobbling out of the medic tent on the arm of his batman, Tobin.

Now, there were six of them left, if Peter's widow was included, and all wondered *was this to be their fate?*

Someone had to speak and break the chain of their morbid, damning thoughts.

"Peter would not want this." Five pairs of morose eyes looked up at Matthias. "We all knew this was likely when we signed up to fight Napoleon."

"How would you want us to feel if it were you?" James asked.

"I would want you to keep going forward and give my life meaning."

"Precisely. We mourn this night and move forward tomorrow. His death shall not be in vain." James said with quiet conviction.

"What about Kitty?" Peter's wife that followed the drum and felt like one of them.

"We see what she wishes to do. I expect she will wish to return home," Matthias answered. He had known her and Peter from the cradle, and was most devastated by the loss.

"The French are worn down, this cannot go on much longer," Luke said, though he would be sent home. No one else dared voice such hope.

"We are worn down," James muttered.

Philip, the quiet, thoughtful one, spoke. "If anything happens to me, will someone see to my sister? She has no one else."

"I swear it," Colin said, leading the others to do the same.

"*Pietas et honos.*"

Philip nodded, too choked up to speak.

"Loyalty and honour," another swore the oath in English.

They returned to silence, each brooding over what had happened and what was yet to come.

CHAPTER 1

England
Summer 1815

*P*erhaps pride had died after all.

It was time to beg for mercy.

Pride had been a vicious master, but something more primitive had killed it at last. Survival. Kitty stood before the gates of the grand estate on the Sussex coast she had once called home, unable to open them. Not much had changed. The manse of golden stone still sat atop the hill overlooking its purview. Perhaps she would think it beautiful if it had not left such a bitter taste in her mouth. But now it seemed like her last chance. No, that wasn't fair; doubtless she could ask one of the other brethren for charity, but if she had to do that it might as well be from here. At least this was familiar. *Better the devil you know.*

Her hands shook as she pushed open the gate and picked up her portmanteau, which held the last of her meagre possessions. *One foot in front of the other*, she ordered herself. It was easy to convince herself she was on any other path as she trudged along that heavily wooded drive up to the house. It was a good two miles from the gate. Memories assailed her of two young boys and a little girl hiding and playing amongst these trees. They had seemed so large to her then. How often had she played fair Guinevere while Peter and Matthias had traded between Sir Lancelot and King Arthur? A slight sigh escaped her lips.

How she had idolized them both! But Peter had been the one to save her. It was that fact that had kept her from crawling back here during the past two years.

He is not here to save you now.

No, she thought bitterly, though she knew it was unfair. Peter had been killed and she had been left behind on her own. She had known before she asked that Peter's family had no love for her. They had objected loudly as had the old earl when Peter had decided to marry her and take her with him.

"We can all be together forever," he had said kindly.

He was not the one she had wanted to marry. It was water under the bridge, she thought as she stopped atop the stone bridge and watched the small stream trickle beneath, her last pair of shoes so thin it was a miracle they had not yet worn a hole through the sole.

More memories beset her where she stopped to rest, of skipping stones when the water had been deep enough, fishing and swimming... It felt like a lifetime ago, though it had only been five years since they had escaped for the Peninsula; two since Peter's death. Now she felt trapped and hopeless again.

She had written to Peter's brother, Sir Nigel, when she returned, but although he had made it clear there was no home for her to be found with Peter's family, he had given her twenty pounds of guilt money. Twenty pounds did not last very long, even with the strictest of economies.

She had learned how to cook and mend whilst following the drum and that had been the only way she had survived thus far. If she'd had family to live with, then perhaps she could have managed. But now, short of selling her body, she had run out of options.

After walking the long drive, she raised her hand to the knocker of what had once been her home. The lion's head watched her as though it would devour her.

The door opened to the face of a stranger. "May I help you?"

This was not at all what she had expected. The butler was to have recognized her, yet a stranger's face stood before her, one of perhaps forty years with dark hair that was barely etched with grey around the ears. As she stood there in her widow's weeds, which were in as poor of shape as her shoes, she began to lose heart.

"I would like to see his lordship," she said, making certain her diction indicated she was a lady even if her appearance did not.

"I am afraid his lordship is not here," the man returned, though not unkindly.

"I should like to wait for him. I have travelled a great distance to speak with him," she pleaded.

"You may be waiting a very long time, ma'am. His lordship is off fighting with His Majesty's army on the Continent."

Kitty grasped her chest. "He went back?"

"Yes, ma'am."

"How could he?" Tears came unbidden to her eyes. He had said at the time of Peter's death that he would also be returning home to take over his duties as Earl. He had also assured her, if she ever needed help, to come there and seek it of him. Yet here she was, and he was back on the Continent, fighting against the horrid Napoleon and risking his life. Had Peter's not been enough?

"I think you had better come in, ma'am," the strange butler said. Kitty was too dismayed to argue and followed him in to the receiving room off the entrance hall. "I will have some refreshments brought to you while you compose yourself," he added and bowed himself out of the room.

What was she to do? Would anyone still know her there? She had no proof of who she was. It had never occurred to her that Matthias would be gone. Suddenly she could not control the tears that fell. She had kept them in for so long they refused to be held back.

"Oh, my poor dear," a kind elderly voice said as the servant set down the tea tray and held out a fine linen handkerchief to Kitty.

"Thank you," she said, trying to control her emotions. She blew her nose and took a deep breath. "Forgive me. I was not expecting his lordship to be absent. He said, if I ever needed anything…" Kitty dried her eyes and looked up. "Mrs. Harlow?" she asked, recognizing the elderly housekeeper, who was still short and stout, now with her familiar top knot completely white and her smile lines deeply etched into her face.

"Miss Kitty?"

"'Tis I." She nodded.

"Why I would not have recognized you!"

"I am in a sad state," she agreed. "Things have not been easy since Peter died."

"I did hear the awful news. I had thought you might return to Willowsbend."

"They did not care to welcome me there. I have been trying to make my way in London."

The housekeeper handed Kitty a cup of tea. "I cannot say I am surprised. Sir Nigel is not the most charitable of gentlemen. What can I help you with? I have no doubt his lordship would wish it."

"He said as much, but I would not have come had I any alternative. I thought perhaps he might find me a position."

"I do not think he would be pleased with that, Miss Kitty." She frowned, using the pet name from Kitty's youth.

"I may be a relation, but a very distant one. I am no longer a ward of the Earls of Thackeray. It was not my lot in life to be a fine lady, after all," she said frankly, without expecting contradiction.

"Mr. Peter would be rolling over in his grave if he knew how you had been treated!" the housekeeper protested.

"He would be appalled to know my position, yet he did not make provision for me. I do not begrudge it. Had it not been for him, I would have been in this position much sooner. He was too young and full of life to have thought he would die young. None of us thought it possible."

The housekeeper dabbed at her own eyes. "And now his lordship has gone back again. I know he felt it were his duty, especially when they asked, because so many men have been sent to America. But with Master Henry being his heir, and him not fit to be lord, if you'll pardon my saying so…I know you understand."

Kitty did. Henry had been wild even as a youth. Apparently he had not mended his ways. "Is there nothing I can do here? I am not too proud, Mrs. Harlow. I can turn my hand at most things now."

"It wouldn't be right, Miss Kitty. His lordship would have my head if he knew. I, myself, am to retire when he returns. My sister and I have purchased a cottage in Exeter and I am to live there with her."

Kitty's heart sank. Mrs. Harlow was her best chance. "Could I not learn your position and keep house? I am a widow, after all. And if Ma —his lordship is upset when he returns, then I will have experience for a post elsewhere."

Mrs. Harlow did not hide her disappointment. "I think it would be best if you just stayed here until his lordship returns, miss. As a guest. You are a *lady*." She emphasized the last word, as if it meant anything.

"Being a lady does not put a roof over my head or food in my mouth or clothes on my back." Her lips trembled and she knew she was pleading. She bit her lower lip. She would not beg.

Warm arms came around her and held her tight. "Oh, Miss Kitty. Not for the world would I send you back out to starve."

∽

MATTHIAS LANDRY, Earl of Thackeray, had never thought to be back on the battlefield. After his best friend Peter had died at Vitoria, he had determined never to fight again. It had been time to take up his duties at Thackeray Close, and if he never smelled nor tasted gunpowder again that would be soon enough for him. However, Napoleon had escaped and all of the experienced officers had been sent to fight in America. What else could he do? How could he sit in his luxurious manor with his abilities whilst young men were dying for their country? If they lost, it might no longer be his anyway.

Now here he was, watching across the valley at Waterloo, facing the vast French army knowing that this would be it; knowing that the day would determine the fate of Europe's democracy.

He could see out over the valley for at least a mile. Each army occupied opposing ridges: the French were spread out in a sea of blue from La Belle-Alliance, and the majority of the Allied Army was hidden from view to the right of the farm, La Haye Sainte, only one brigade fully exposed.

Looking over the faces of his men, he saw some were not even old enough to earn that distinction, with their faces smooth as a babe's. Yet they were willing to fight, even though frightened to death. Matthias had not fought since that day at Vitoria, but it all immediately came back to him as though he had never left.

Peter. So happy and full of life, gone in an instant.

What had become of Kitty? He had tried to help her, but it had been difficult to find her. She had been at Philip's wedding, but something had not been right. He had noticed her clothing had been darned in many places and she was much too thin, but she was also far too proud. He had asked her if she needed anything—if she was happy —but she had smiled falsely and said everything was well. Of course nothing had been right since Peter had married her and they had gone to the Peninsula together. Kitty was his one regret. Matthias should have fought his father better, at the very least insured she would be provided for.

He would find her when he returned.

He needed to rectify his wrongs for it had been he who had ruined everything. They had been the best of friends when Kitty had come to live with them as a girl—better friends than he and his wastrel brother had ever been. But then, when she began to change, Matthias's interest in the girl blossoming into a beautiful woman had been noticed by his father. He should have stood up for her. Instead, Peter had.

Henry would also need to be dealt with when Matthias returned. They'd had a row as Matthias was leaving again just as Henry had been sent down for the term for gambling. He had arrived at the Close, petulant and wanting money. Henry's selfish and spoiled behaviour had struck a nerve—Matthias had threatened to enlist him as a soldier—so his profligate heir had turned tail and stormed from the house. What he should do was marry and produce his own heir, which brought his thoughts back to Kitty...

If he closed his eyes, he could still see her their last happy day together, wisps of her hair blowing in the warm summer breeze, warm amber eyes looking at him like he was the only other person in the world. Kitty, whose smile was brighter than the sun, whose laughter warmed him from the inside out and could charm him from his stoicism, who had stolen his heart and ruined it for any other.

A shout of laughter jolted him back to the present; to a calm, airy peace before Hell ascended to earth.

The first canon shot's scream echoed through the damp, muggy morning; time pausing before the explosion hit the earth and shook it. The only thoughts he would have for the rest of the day would be for survival.

Matthias led his regiment in charge after charge. Many of the British cavalry busied themselves chasing the less experienced French soldiers back and forth across the slope and dispensing with the easier victims. There were numerous knots of French soldiers who formed rallying squares to fend off the British cavalry. As the battle raged on, the losses to his brigade were becoming heavy. Matthias watched soldier after soldier fall before him and forced himself to go on.

The air had become so thick with smoke from gunfire that it was difficult to see or breathe. A fierce fire raged to the west at the Château Hougoumont, making the conditions worse. He forced himself to stop for a drink and to rally his men.

The carnage was unfathomable. When there was an occasional break in the fog and smoke, all that could be seen were thousands upon thousands of human bodies and horses, lying mangled atop each other in mud and blood. It was hard to be out there fighting, to watch his brethren struggle while forcing them to continue.

Then, when it appeared there was nowhere left to fight, another charge would come over what looked to be impossible terrain. It was

sweltering in the heat and humidity, and almost unmanageably difficult to see whom you were fighting.

Searing pain shot through his leg and he fought to control his
horse as a French cuirassier charged at him with a bayonet to finish
him off. He refused to die so easily. Not like Peter. They had to hold
the line to keep the infantry protected. Matthias would not fail his
men. He reached for his pistol, knowing he would not survive hand to
hand combat for long.

He took aim and felled the rider, then saw a bayonet raised at
James. He managed to fend the Frog off until James could handle him,
then Matthias could barely hold his mount when he reached safety
behind the infantry squares to go in search of the sawbones.

CHAPTER 2

*M*rs. Harlow insisted Kitty sleep in one of the guest rooms. It seemed intrusive, but as none of the family were in residence, she gave in and chose her old bedchamber. Little had changed since she had been there as a girl. The walls were still papered in a pink and cream striped paper, and the carpet and coverlet were in matching hues, although they had faded over the years. Some of her dolls sat on a table in the corner just as she had left them.

It might now be a bit shabby with age, but she was flooded with memories and it felt like home.

Home. It was something she had not felt in years. There was no such thing while following the drum and since she had returned to England, she had rented small rooms in the most respectable boarding house she could afford and shared with several other women.

There had been no time to grieve—she had moved from surviving in an army camp to trying to survive in London. It seemed as though the city was full of people desperate for work. She had spent the first year trying to find respectable employment as a governess or a companion, but it had proved impossible to be hired without a personal connection or reference. As the money from Peter's brother had begun to dwindle, she had worked as a seamstress, but it did not bring in enough to pay for both rent and food.

When she had finally become desperate enough to consider selling her body, she had swallowed her pride and decided to beg for work at Thackeray Close.

Now she was in that very house, with a warm bed and food, but she felt guilty for it. She had no right to such luxury. The words still sounded in her head as though it were yesterday: *Ungrateful traitor.*

Regardless of what Mrs. Harlow thought, Kitty determined she would learn to carry out the duties of a housekeeper. That way, Matthias—she must remember to think of him as his lordship—would have no reason not to employ her when he returned.

The next morning, Kitty was up early. Sleeping late was only for the rich and it had been years since she had thought herself anywhere near that status. She was intent on learning everything from Mrs. Harlow, irrespective of how the housekeeper felt about it.

She went to the housekeeper's rooms and knocked on the door. "Good morning, Mrs. Harlow."

"Miss Kitty! You should not be in the servants' quarters."

"I will not be swayed, Mrs. Harlow. What harm would it do to teach me how to manage a household?"

She shook her head. "His lordship will not be pleased, Miss Kitty, but I suppose I could show you a few things. If you remarry, you might have need to run a large establishment."

"Thank you," Kitty said, with more relief than she could express. "Perhaps you should call me Mrs. Gordon now."

The housekeeper eyed her in a sideways fashion. "You do know that name will cause more of a stir than aught else?"

"Perhaps Sir Nigel should have thought of that before he refused to house me."

The housekeeper fought back a smile. "Some might say it would serve him right, I suppose. Very well, come along then. Every morning, I make my rounds to ensure all the servants are awake and performing their duties. The fires must be lit in the winter and the chamber pots emptied before the family awakens."

Kitty knew this from being one of them.

"Cook oversees matters in the kitchens, of course, but we work together if there is a large dinner. We have not had one of those in years, though I will do my best to ensure that you are ready for one. The butler, Mr. Hayes, oversees all the servants, including myself, but he is new enough that he gives me no trouble," Mrs. Harlow said with a mischievous smile.

She led Kitty up the stairs to the linen closet. "Linens are counted every week, after all the chambers are aired and linens washed."

"Even the empty ones?" Kitty asked.

"Even the empty ones," Mrs. Harlow confirmed.

They went back down the stairs to the receiving rooms, where maids were busy dusting and taking carpets outside to be beaten. Mrs. Harlow looked on with approval before taking Kitty back to her rooms.

"My other main duty is going over the menus with his lordship, when he is here. He has always been easy to please and is happy with most anything I suggest." She showed Kitty a list of meals that she rotated through, and even Kitty recognized several of Matthias's favourites.

"When none of the family are in residence, Cook takes care of feeding the servants."

She waved Kitty into a seat in her small sitting room, which was cozy with pink papered walls, embroidered pillows covering the chairs and shelves of trinkets. "That is the sum of it."

Kitty looked at her with suspicion. "That cannot be all."

"I am afraid it is. The house is well run, I say with no small measure of pride."

"It always has been," Kitty agreed. "Perhaps I could assist you with some of your duties?"

The housekeeper looked a little disgruntled. Kitty knew she was trying to fob her off, but she would be persistent.

"I suppose the still-room would benefit from some attention. The herb garden does not thrive as it did when her ladyship had it in her care. You used to help her with it, did you not?"

"Help is a very generous term. I fear I was never possessed of her skill."

The housekeeper rose and went to the small room situated down one of the passages near the kitchen, where the herbs and medicinal powders were kept. Kitty had fond memories of the Countess, of how she had attended the smaller garden and lovingly prepared tinctures and poultices when needed. It had been her hobby as well as one of the time-honoured duties of the mistress of the house.

Kitty inhaled deeply. The stone-walled room had not lost the familiar earthy and medicinal scent.

"Her book is still here," Mrs. Harlow said as she reached for a leather-bound journal lying on a shelf. "Sadly, I have no skill in herbalism. Jenkins keeps the weeds from the garden, of course, but that is the extent of it."

Kitty took the book. "I helped to tend the wounded and sick on occasion, when necessary. Many of the wives did; but I am no doctor."

"Of course not, but housekeepers need some knowledge of the still-room."

"Of course," Kitty agreed as the housekeeper neatly left her alone with the task. Kitty had little doubt that the herb garden was in pristine condition, but if caring for its produce kept her employed and with a roof over her head until Matthias returned, then so be it.

As she had suspected, everything was neat and orderly in the room —jars arranged tidily on the shelves, pestles and mortars stacked together on the work bench and the cabinets well stocked with the phials and other paraphernalia of the herbalist's art. Many more of the herbs made sense to her now, though. She fingered a jar of willow bark tea and knew it was used to keep fevers down after infections. Many soldiers died of infections, she recalled. At least Peter had not suffered. He had been shot from his horse and had died instantly. She put the jar back in its place and decided to go and look at the garden. It was hard not to think of Peter and Matthias here, with all their vivacity now gone. She could only hope and pray that Matthias would return again, unharmed, although no one who had any part of war was ever the same again.

It was a warm July day, and the bees were buzzing about their business as she strolled through the garden. A large hedge of hawthorn made a wall of protection around the cherished herbs and plants her ladyship had cultivated. The lavender immediately caught Kitty's eye, still fragrant and abundant as it had been before. It had always been her favourite, with its bright purple colours and unique scent.

She sat on the bench in the centre of the garden and opened the Countess' book across her lap to learn what she could. Perhaps Mrs. Harlow would give her this task only for now, but she would do it well and hopefully be entrusted with more soon.

As she read about each plant and its medicinal properties, she found it in the garden and learned what she could about it. If something was in low supply, then she would harvest it and prepare it as written. She started at the first row, and looked up the plants by their neatly labelled placards.

The Chamomile flower is used in tea for sleep or as a compress to reduce dropsy. It is also beneficial for all types of agues. It takes away weariness and eases pains.

Kitty looked with some scepticism at the small white and yellow flower that resembled a daisy. "You sound like a miracle for such a plain little flower," she said dryly before moving on.

Feverfew also comes from the daisy family and a syrup may be made up for the winter months. The mixture is good for the stuffiness of the chest and for cough. It is also useful for cleansing of the wound after childbirth, vertigo, taking away freckles...

"Again, it sounds like a miracle."

St John's wort is a pretty yellow flowering bush. Its properties are singularly useful for wounds and bruising on the inside and out. The seed is useful for sciatica and palsy.

Had the sawbones on the Peninsula known of St. John's wort, she wondered as she closed the book. Three herbs were enough to learn for now. Who even knew if this new-found knowledge was to be needed?

Kitty sat back and lifted her face to the warm sun. She could use some of the feverfew on her new freckles later, she thought devilishly. Not that she had given her looks any thought for quite some time. Poor people had little time for vanity. She had not felt as free as this in years. There were still many obstacles to overcome, such as convincing Mrs. Harlow and Matthias, but at least for now she had a reprieve.

It was hard not to think of Peter, now that she was back here where they had all grown up together. How would he feel about her being here again now?

She owned to a definite ache of longing and remembrance for him as a result of returning to where she had so many memories: memories of him and of Matthias, memories she had thrust to the back of her mind and locked tightly away.

Kitty registered carriage wheels coming up the drive, but as it would hardly be anyone to call upon her, she paid it little mind. Since no family was in residence, she mused, it was probably only a delivery.

She enjoyed the sunshine for another half an hour before gathering her bonnet and book and returning to the house.

To her surprise, the upper servants were scurrying about carrying pails of water, blankets and towels. Mrs. Harlow was giving orders to others and two footmen were carrying trunks up the stairs.

What was happening? Kitty wondered at the activity but stayed near the wall where she was out of the way. She would know soon enough.

She could hear voices; cultured male accents speaking with Hayes in the main doorway, clearly before their owners' departure. To her chagrin, she was unable to catch a glimpse of who they were from her vantage point behind the stairs.

Just then, Mrs. Harlow began walking towards her across the entrance hall and Kitty finally stepped forward to ask.

"Has someone arrived?" she asked.

"Oh, Miss Kitty, 'tis the master! He has come home and he's in a very bad way."

"What do you mean?" Kitty whispered, but from the look on Mrs. Harlow's face, she knew the answer.

"The Duke of Waverley has brought him here but could not stay. The master was shot at that battle of Waterloo by the French and he's unconscious with a fever. There was a nurse here with him as well and she did not know if he would live." Her last word caught on a sob. "Forgive me. I am only just now taking a moment to catch my breath."

Kitty knew how that was. It was better to stay busy. "What may I do to help?"

The housekeeper shook her head. "Sit with the master, if you have a stomach for the sick bed. His man has come back with him and he seems to know what to do, but I am sure he would welcome the help. Dr. Beverly has been sent for."

Kitty nodded and walked towards the stairs, her insides gripped with fear. She climbed slowly, as if answering the death knell, not knowing what would be on the other side waiting. *Please, God, no. I cannot take another loss. I need him.* A world without Matthias and Peter was not a world she wanted to inhabit.

By the time she reached the top of the stairs, she heard the doctor's arrival. Not yet ready to be confronted with someone from the past when her emotions were so conflicted, she stepped into the room next door to the Earl's to wait. Loud footsteps echoed through the entrance chamber of the house. Each loud, booted step seemed to have silenced the household as collectively its inhabitants waited for the proclamation.

"How long has he been like this?" The doctor's voice boomed when he entered the bedchamber. Kitty could hear him opening his bag; something chinked, as though he was drawing instruments out.

"Nigh a month." Hornsby, Matthias's batman from the army answered. "The nurse who tended him was an angel on earth. He 'as been delirious fer at least the past two weeks."

"It is a wonder he is still alive," the doctor answered, with a little huff. "This is the only wound?"

"Yes, sir," Hornsby replied. "The sawbones in the field dug the bullet out."

"It appears to be clean enough. There is little I can do for him now. It is too late to let him. The wound has already suppurated and poisoned his blood. It is up to God, now."

Hornby muttered something Kitty could not make out.

"Here are some morphine drops to keep him comfortable, and bathe him in ice when the fevers rage. Send for me if he awakens."

That was all? Kitty did not care to do nothing. Perhaps there was something she could do to help. She listened and waited until she was certain Dr. Beverly had gone, then steeled herself to look upon Matthias.

Taking a deep breath, she left her sanctum, stepped forward to the Earl's threshold and tapped lightly on the open door. Hornsby looked up and met her gaze. He did not recognize her. His head bald and his skin weathered made him look a bit daunting combined with his size. Had she not known his was a rough exterior with a soft middle, she might have been intimidated.

"I am here to help." She did not wait for a response, though Hornsby grumbled about not needing help. She moved towards Matthias whether she had intended to or no; nothing short of an army could have stopped her.

His eye sockets were sunken, his lips dry and cracked, skin flushed with the heat caused by fever. He was clean and still in repose for the moment, looking like an angel sleeping despite his obvious state of infirmity. His once light blonde hair had now darkened a little with age, and his features, once boyish, were now chiselled into a finely sculptured face and jaw.

"He is exhausted from the journey. It wasn't an easy one. But this calm won't last. The general way of things is fits of delirium and gibberish, with thrashing and whole body tremors from the chills."

Kitty nodded absently. She knew exactly of what he spoke, having seen it time and again in the field hospitals. She could not stop her hand from reaching up to smooth his brow. "You are not allowed to leave me, too, Matthias Landry," she whispered, her chin trembling.

"He's as tough as nails, ma'am. He won't die now after the fight he's put up," Hornsby said gruffly. Doubtless he was as afraid as Kitty was.

"Peter did not have the chance to fight," she said to herself.

"Mrs. Gordon, is that you?"

Kitty nodded and looked up at the batman. "I am here to assume Mrs. Harlow's position when she retires."

Hornsby frowned, but did not say anything. *Praise be*, she thought. A maid entered with some barley water and ice, and set the tray on the night table beside the bed. Hornsby inclined his head to Kitty and then moved over to try the broth also on the tray.

"Allow me. I have not yet had the chance to help." It should have been she who had been at Matthias' bedside instead of some nurse he did not know. But she was there now.

Hornsby held up Matthias's head as Kitty pried open his mouth and dribbled some broth between his lips until he swallowed.

"Exhausting work, that it is, but we have been managing some," Hornsby remarked. They continued in that fashion until the bowl was empty. At least Matthias was drinking. It was some small measure of comfort.

"What do you need? Do you require any herbs or medicines besides morphine?" Kitty asked, half out of desperation.

"We ran out of everything on the ship coming over. Miss Murphy was giving him willow bark for the fevers, that I do know."

"We have plenty of that. I will go and prepare some at once. And the wound?"

Hornsby shrugged. "It appears to have healed. Anything wrong seems to be on the inside."

Kitty hurried down to the still-room, grateful for a way to be useful. How much longer would this situation continue? How long could a person live with such a fever?

When she returned, Matthias had gone into crisis. Hornsby was trying to cover him with ice, but Matthias was thrashing violently about the bed, the sheets tangled about his limbs. He was drenched with sweat, yet also in the grip of bone-shattering chills.

"We must get some willow bark into him!" Kitty said with urgency as she hastened to help.

"I'll do my best to hold him for you, Mrs. Gordon, but you see what it is."

Kitty leaned down to Matthias's ear. "Matthias, 'tis Kitty. You must help us. Please take the medicine." Pleading probably did little good, but anything was worth trying. It was their last chance.

Hornsby held Matthias as best he was able, and Kitty poured the saline draught slowly into her old playmate's mouth; some Matthias was able to swallow and much dribbled down his chin. Then they untangled him from his sheets and worked to hold ice on him as best they could.

"What else can we do?" Hornsby asked, desperation lacing his voice.

Kitty shook her head. "Keep this up as long as we must."

"This is not the time!" Mrs. Harlow's voice sounded shrilly just before the door burst open.

"Let me see him!"

"Master Henry!" Mrs. Harlow scolded, coming into the room right behind the newcomer.

Kitty was so upset she could not even look up at Matthias' brother. She kept her head down and tried to compose herself before speaking.

"He is going to die, isn't he? I could not believe it without seeing it."

"He is very ill, sir," Hornsby answered.

Without another word, Henry left in the same whirl in which he had entered.

CHAPTER 3

*M*atthias awoke and he did not know where he was. If he did not know better, he would think he had been ill with a fever. Besides feeling like he'd been trampled by a horse, he'd also felt he was walking through the fires of hell. At times, he had had the strangest dreams, as though he were on a battlefield or in the field hospital, perhaps even on a boat and then in a carriage. Now, however, he felt as though he were at home in his own bed. He struggled to open his eyes; his lids were heavy. The dark green canopy was there, just as he had suspected. The smells were familiar so he could not say precisely what they were—the Close had its own scent—like home. The sounds were that of the country, with the birds chirping as though the world was as it ought to be. But he knew better. Yes, he was home, but how did he come to be there?

He closed his eyes tight as a flood of memories washed over him. He had been shot in the leg but had managed to reach the sawbones. He attempted to move his leg and felt pain, but did that mean it was still there? He was afraid to look. Like all soldiers, he had heard story after story of the mysterious phantom pain where limbs hurt even after they had been amputated.

The time between then and now was a blur. He remembered the

ELIZABETH JOHNS

bullet being extracted and glimpses of Tobin and Philip, Luke and James. Where was Colin?

He remembered his vow properly to take care of Kitty. It seemed strange that he should think of her in this moment, but she had been his last thought before he had been wounded, had she not? Peter would have been very disappointed to know Matthias had not looked after her properly. *Pietas et honos.*

She had been his responsibility, not Peter's, but Peter had done the honourable thing before Matthias had, and now he had failed her yet again. She had denied it at Philip's wedding, when Matthias had asked how she was, if she needed anything, but he was the one who knew her best and he had allowed her pride to win.

Regret overwhelmed him.

Supposing he was a cripple? Somehow, in his heart, he knew he was not the same but God had decided to let him live, for whatever reason. He was not certain if he had the strength of character to do so with good grace. After a moment, he opened his eyes to see the truth of his fears. He felt as though a new chapter in his life was beginning, but reflected dolefully it was doubtless one of the ones in the middle that tended to lead somewhere else in the story. Those were never his favourite. While he enjoyed meeting the characters in the beginning, he sometimes flipped to the pages at the end to discover what happened to them. He been told many times it was a grievous flaw in his character. Perhaps he was to be taught a lesson: that the story was the journey. It occurred to him that having studied law, perhaps all the dry reading had ruined him for reading simply for pleasure. He suspected he was about to discover all about journeys.

He threw back his coverlet and attempted to sit up, quickly discovering that he was as weak as a new-born calf and likely as awkward. Pain seared through his leg and he dared to look down. It was still attached. Thank God. At least, he thought he was grateful. He should probably reserve judgement until he attempted to use it. He pulled back his fresh nightshirt, noting how remarkably clean he was. No doubt his batman, Hornsby, had come with him, the stubborn fool.

His leg was covered in a dressing from hip to knee. Nonetheless,

22

he needed to see the damage despite the searing pain when he tried to lift his knee in order to unwind the linen strips. He gritted his teeth but was forced to lie back from his exertions, a cold sweat creeping over his brow. How long had he been ill, that he was so debilitated? Had they defeated Bonaparte on that fateful day? Something in his vague memories told him they had. Was the assurance from whispered conversations? It mattered not. At least this action had been for a purpose. Flashes of the battle and the carnage came vividly to his recollection. So much blood; so much death. The sounds were as loud and the smells as pungent as if he were there. He prayed it had not been in vain.

He leaned forward again, determined to see the remnants of the day upon his body. It was strange; a wound to be sure, but it was as though he were looking at someone else's leg.

He touched the oddly puckered skin, which was mildly warm although his leg felt little sensation.

The feeling, or lack thereof, was enough to raise the bile in his throat. Turning away, he resolved to get out of the bed.

Shifting to the edge nearly exhausted him. He had not survived this long only to fail now. He slid down to put weight on his feet, lifting himself from the bed at the same time. The injured leg collapsed beneath him and he was not in time to catch himself. As he toppled to the floor, his body made a resounding thump. The pain that shot through his leg indicated it might be broken, but how would he know?

The chamber door burst open and Hornsby looked first at the bed and then the floor with alarm. "My lord! Why did you try to get out of bed?" he admonished.

"It is good to see you, too, Hornsby. I wanted to see how damaged my leg was. Is it broken?"

The batman frowned. "I could not say. I suppose it is possible. A bullet was lodged in the bone, I believe, but the surgeon said nothing about a break."

"It is infected, I presume?" Matthias asked.

"Yes, my lord. It has been over a month since we left Brussels."

Matthias gave a distracted nod. He had missed an entire month? "I only have vague recollections."

"The Duke of Waverley brought you and Lieutenant O'Neill back on his private yacht." The batman swallowed hard and looked away.

"What is it? Did Tobin die?"

"No, my lord. At least he was alive when we parted. However, Major White was killed on the battlefield."

Matthias closed his eyes and tipped his head back. Colin was one of his best men and dearest friends. He remembered. Colin had taken charge when Matthias fell out.

"It was swift, my lord. It took him and his horse together instantly."

Matthias nodded. That was every soldier's hope if he did not remain unscathed. A swift death was better than being left maimed. Was that to be his fate? Would it have been better if he had also died?

"Let me put you back in the bed, sir," Hornsby said, moving to lift Matthias.

"No. I have been in a bed for a month. I will sit in the chair by the window."

The batman helped him to his good foot and he hobbled a few feet to the chair, leaning heavily on his man.

That exertion alone felt as though he had fought in a hard battle all day.

"I shall send for the doctor, my lord. He asked to be informed when you awoke."

"Then I want a proper meal," Matthias said. "I feel as weak as a kitten."

"I am not surprised. We have been spooning barley water and broth down you but that is not enough to sustain a man's strength."

Matthias had just finished a proper beef steak and coddled eggs when the doctor arrived. Doctor Beverly had been taking care of the Landry family for decades. He was a short and round gentleman, with a balding head and a kind face.

"Good morning, my lord. It is good to see you awake." He glanced towards the empty tray with scant traces of his meal. "I see you have a healthy appetite, though I would have advised caution and a bland diet."

Matthias inclined his head. "I have never been one to be a good invalid. I believe I must eat hearty in order to return to normal."

The doctor looked sceptical, but held his tongue. "I should like to examine your leg, my lord. The wound is mostly healed, but having not extracted the bullet myself, and with you being so ill with fever, it was difficult to determine the extent of your injuries."

"You mean how handicapped I will be?" Matthias preferred plain speaking.

He nodded. "It is a miracle you survived the infection. Battlefield medicine is an abomination."

"They do the best they can. I would not wish to be a sawbones in the field," Matthias admitted. He had never thought much about what it must be like to try to save thousands of wounded men pouring into the medical tent, and having to decide who was worth saving and who would be left to die.

"They do not even wash their instruments between patients!" Dr. Beverly's face reflected his horror. "At least, that is what I have heard," he added.

"I cannot say I was of a mind to notice at the time."

"You were taken back to a house in Brussels and a nurse there cleaned out the wound and poured a large amount of spirits into it. She was convinced the spirits served to kill the infection," Hornsby explained.

"Who am I to argue, since I am still alive?"

Dr. Beverly humphed. "That is probably due to the strength of your humours."

Whatever those were, Matthias thought sardonically. Most medicine was all but witchcraft in his opinion. "Is there a chance the bone is broken? When I tried to stand, I felt a searing pain before it collapsed beneath me."

"The bone could have fractured on impact," the doctor agreed. He examined the leg as Matthias winced with pain. "The outside appears to be healing well. We could place a splint against it for few weeks, to help the bone knit properly, though you might not walk again as you once did."

"Anything is worth a try," Matthias answered, unwilling to consider that as an option.

"At least they did not amputate in the field," the doctor said gallantly. "I will fetch a splint from my trap and some laudanum for the pain."

"They would have done," Hornsby admitted. "Lieutenant O'Neill would not hear of it and we removed you to Brussels."

"It seems I am indebted to Lieutenant O'Neill."

"Aye, and the nurse. 'Twas O'Neill who took you to Miss Murphy."

"Then I shall write to him, if you will be so good as to bring me my travelling desk and some brandy. And don't be watering it, either."

"Yes, my lord," the batman said, ignoring Matthias' jibe and, collecting the tray, heading for the door.

"Oh, and Hornsby?"

He turned back.

"Have you heard anything from Mrs. Gordon? I thought perhaps one of the brethren might have mentioned her."

~

ON THE POINT OF ENTERING, Kitty stood outside the door, halted by Matthias's words. She had been helping to care for him over the past week or two—how long had it been? The days slipped by in a rhythm and time seemed to have no meaning.

Something had given her pause and Hornsby had been looking directly at her when Matthias had asked about her. She shook her head vehemently and held her finger to her lips. It was too soon. He still needed to heal and she was not certain of his reaction, not to mention the fact she still had not convinced Mrs. Harlow that she was up to the task of housekeeper. Now that Matthias was home she had doubts herself.

But what would he say when he found out she had been here all along?

The doctor returned with the splint as Kitty began to walk down the hall.

"Miss Kitty?" the doctor asked, recognizing her. His voice seemed to reverberate through the house.

"Dr. Beverly, how good to see you." She bobbed a slight curtsy and then hurried away, hoping he would forget he had seen her by the time he reached Matthias's room.

She hurried down the stairs and almost ran into Mrs. Harlow.

"What is the matter, Miss Kitty? You look as though you've seen a ghost."

"No, not a ghost. His lordship appears to have awakened, and his fever has broken."

"Praise the heavens!" the housekeeper exclaimed.

"Yes, indeed." Perhaps this would work only if she could bring herself to speak to Matthias. Had she truly thought she could be his servant? She had not thought, truth be told. She was hungry and desperate and her only thoughts had been for her next meal and a roof over her head.

How quickly she had allowed herself to become comfortable here again! If only Matthias had stayed away longer, what would've happened? It was a very good thing he'd come home to remind her of her place. If only she knew what that was.

"Miss Kitty?"

She had not realized the housekeeper was still there watching her. She started and looked at the woman.

"Was he pleased to see you?"

"I did not enter the room. The doctor is tending to him." She swallowed hard and bit her lower lip, fighting back tears.

"Now, none of that, Miss Kitty. His lordship survived the fever, he will survive whatever lies ahead."

She nodded, grateful Mrs. Harlow had partially misunderstood, because no one truly understood her plight. She inhaled deeply and firmed her resolve. "I think you would be well served to proceed with training me to take over your duties. Now that his lordship is home, you may have your well-deserved retirement."

Mrs. Harlow stood tall as though offended. "As if I would leave his lordship at a time like this!"

"I had no thought to hasten you out of the door. I only meant that you must not pretend any longer I am to be a lady. I know you have been trying to fob me off." She eyed the elderly woman, who had the grace to look guilty.

"'Tis not right, and I know his lordship will agree with me."

Kitty did not agree with her but held her tongue. "I shall not broach the topic with him until he is more recovered."

"And when do you mean to tell him you are here?" the housekeeper asked knowingly. "You cannot keep your presence a secret from him."

"I do not intend to. I will speak to him when Dr. Beverly leaves."

"Very well. If he agrees to this mad scheme, then you may assume my duties."

Kitty nodded and watched Mrs. Harlow disappear through one of the solid oak doors that led to the bowels of the house.

She stood in the panelled hallway where the banister curved upwards to the family apartments, a portrait of the old Earl looking down upon her with a disapproving scowl upon his face. Closing her eyes, she heard again the laughter from when the old Earl had been away and she and the boys had slid down the polished rail, their only concern that Nurse would not catch them in the act. The old butler, Percy, had aided and abetted them whenever he thought no one was looking. A most superior individual in many ways, he had always been kind to them. She smiled at the memory. How had things gone so wrong?

Could she truly live here again as though nothing had ever happened? Or was it better to ask for charity and leave, never to return again?

She thought of how cruel the world was for those who must make their own way in it. There were women who made a good living, of course, but Kitty was caught between two worlds—neither a lady nor a servant. Perhaps it had been a mistake to think she would ever be accepted as such here, although it might be possible to obtain a reference from Matthias. That was what had been lacking when she had sought work as a governess or companion.

Approaching footsteps disturbed her thoughts and she looked up to see Hornsby coming down the stairs with the doctor.

She turned and forced a smile, knowing she could not escape this time. "How is he, Doctor?"

"He survived the fever, so I trust there should be no more danger on that front." He hesitated.

She looked at the batman and frowned.

"However, his leg might have more damage than we first thought," the doctor said. "If the bone is shattered it might never heal properly. Only time will tell if it must come off; much will depend on whether or not more infection sets in. In the meantime I have splinted it and I will call again in a few days unless you have need of me. Should you have any concerns, then send someone for me." He placed his hat on his head. "It is nice to see you home again, Miss Kitty."

She smiled and nodded and watched him leave before then turning back to Hornsby. "Will he not walk again?"

"I don't rightly know, ma'am. The leg collapsed on him when he tried to stand."

"Perhaps that is only weakness. He has been in bed for over a month!" She tried to reason, as much for herself as for him. The thought of Matthias as anything less than whole and vibrant was difficult. He had always been so strong, so alive, so... dashing.

"He be right determined," Hornsby said, as if he also could not think of his master as anything other than what he had been before. "He asked me to post these letters. He is looking for you," the batman went on, in a mild accusatory tone.

"Do not post them yet. I will speak with him."

He gave her a look that would be impertinent were it not well deserved. Matthias had become his master first... and if she intended to become a servant, she would be his equal.

"This is not easy for me, Hornsby. I was brought up here as a ward of the old Earl."

Understanding crossed his face. Had he not known? "I only knew you as Mrs. Gordon. I did not know of the connection."

She had assumed as much, but she hated to see the pity in his eyes.

"What are you afraid of? He has been worrying about you."

"That I cannot say," she answered vaguely. She could hardly put everything into words. Not many knew the full history between Matthias and herself and it felt disloyal to Peter to say anything. "I will go and speak with him now."

The batman gave a nod and Kitty turned to the banister, knowing this was something she had to do. The longer she put it off, the harder it would be to leave if he denied her.

As she climbed the stairs, she debated what to say. By the time she reached Matthias' door, she still had not decided. It stood open a crack and she knocked lightly. There was no answer. Had he perhaps fallen asleep already from the exertions with the doctor?

She peeked inside, and saw him lying in repose, as peaceful as an angel. It was hard to believe only a few hours before he'd been knocking on death's door. She turned to leave, feeling like an intruder. She wasn't ready.

"Kitty?"

She stepped warily through the door. Had he seen her staring at him? Her cheeks burned with embarrassment.

"I must be dreaming again, or else had too much brandy," he said to himself.

"You are not dreaming," she answered quietly turning back to him.

He held out his hand and she walked into the room to stand at his bedside.

"How did you know I was here? Or did you somehow know I wanted to find you?"

"Why?" she asked.

His light green eyes were the same as they always been, though now with slight wrinkles around the edges seasoned by life and war. He looked away towards the window. "Because I needed to."

What did that mean? She did not speak her thoughts, but waited.

"I have never felt easy about what happened and then you refused my help after Peter's death."

She could not deny it.

"Will you let me help you now?"

"You asked why I was here. I came to ask for a position. Mrs. Harlow is ready to retire." There, she had said it and waited for his response. *What must it be like to hold someone's fate in your hands?*

CHAPTER 4

*M*atthias could not have been more relieved that Kitty had come. For a moment, he was able to simply be glad and forget about his injuries, Peter's death and what had led to Kitty becoming married and then a young widow. Reality, however, quickly came crashing down. "I cannot allow you to be my servant, Kitty."

"Being your housekeeper would be a vast improvement over the last two years, I assure you."

He turned to look at her then, and suddenly he saw more than perhaps he wanted to. Those fathomless amber eyes did not hide the hurt and abandonment she felt. "Peter did not provide for you." It was a statement, not a question.

"He did not expect to die," she countered.

"And Sir Nigel?"

"He gave me twenty pounds to leave and pretend we were not acquainted."

Matthias cursed and did not bother to apologize. He knew she had heard much worse as an army wife. "What would you do if you had the funds?"

"That is a moot question," she said quietly.

"I swore to Peter that I would look after you. All the brethren did. Why did you not say anything to me?" It hurt more than he would like to admit.

"I am here now, my lord."

"My lord? Is that what we have come to? We were brought up as brother and sister." He knew the words to be untrue as he spoke them.

"Not quite brother and sister," she said sharply.

No, not quite brother and sister in the end. His father had thought she had had ambitions to be a future countess and had thrown her out.

He wanted to pace the room and run his hands through his hair. He had never been a good invalid and he desperately wanted to be out of this bed. "What would you have me do, Kitty?" he finally asked.

"Must I grovel? You need a housekeeper and I know this house better than anyone else. Over the past few weeks I have been learning from Mrs. Harlow, even though she thinks it is beneath me."

"It is!" he shouted.

"I would rather be here than a governess or a companion to some demanding mistress!"

"I will give you what you want, Kitty. A cottage? An allowance? You need not lower yourself."

"Indeed, this would be raising myself considerably. I do not want your pity, my lord. There is no shame in work."

"People will talk."

"They will gossip, I have no doubt, but that does not matter. I am a widow, not a young miss any longer."

Matthias had not been expecting this, and he did not care for it one bit. He was too tired to think of all the objections as he should. Nevertheless, he opened his mouth to argue, but Kitty stayed him with her hand. "Please think on it before you refuse. If nothing else, Mrs. Harlow should be allowed to retire. You could take me on for a probationary period and if I fail, I will leave without another word."

Nothing at all could have caused him to predict the situation. Kitty had not been brought up to be a housekeeper, but a lady wife. His wife.

He shook his head. "You are young, Kitty. You should find another husband." He hated saying those words. How they tasted like ash on his tongue!

"You think that is all I am fit for?"

"'Twas not what I meant, and you know it." At least they were now arguing like brother and sister.

"I know nothing except that you offered to help me. This is a perfect solution. You need a housekeeper and I need a position. I will engage to stay out of your way if that is your wish."

"My wish is for my leg to be healed so I can get out of this deuced bed!" He threw one of his pillows across the room in a fit of pique and then fell back on the bed with exhaustion.

"Perhaps this was a mistake," she said quietly. "I do not know what I was expecting when I came here, but I did not know where else to go."

"You do not need to leave. You know I will always take care of you even if I have not done a good job of it thus far."

"I was not your responsibility, and I am not now. I may be borrowing on our past relationship in asking for a position, but I do not ask for any special favours hereafter. I do not know what I expected when Peter and I married and followed the drum, but I am not the same girl who left here."

Matthias turned to meet her gaze. She was certainly no girl any longer. She already looked better than when last he had seen her; her face was no longer gaunt and she wore a better gown, even if it was dove grey. That colour did not really suit anyone, did it? Was it the colour or was it the indication of mourning or of servitude? He wanted to see her in bright hues again with the happiness and laughter that had resonated through the house during the old times before. She was still beautiful, but she was not his.

He moved to change position and nearly doubled over in pain. A cold sweat broke out over his skin.

Kitty was instantly by his side. "What is it? How can I help?"

"'Tis nothing," he snapped.

"It is not nothing. I helped with the wounded after battles; I even helped with you."

Turning, he glared at her to cover his surprise.

She continued, "The doctor mentioned the bone might even be broken. If you need help, there is no shame in asking."

How could he explain to her? He did not trouble himself to try.

"You can help by filling my glass." He inclined his head towards the bedside table where a bottle of brandy sat.

"The doctor left laudanum drops." She held them up and he knocked them from her hand.

"No!" The dreams—the nightmares those caused. He could not look her in the eye, but she very likely had her own.

He saw her nod and then pick up the offending bottle from where he had thrown it on the floor.

Kitty poured him some brandy but with a look of disapproval. She poured only a small amount into the glass—barely half—and handed it to him.

"Thank you," he said, hearing the surliness in his voice. He just wanted to be left to bear his pain in private.

"Shall I send Hornsby up since you will not let me help?"

"There is nothing you can do. I will be bedridden for weeks to come and only time will tell what the damage is."

"I am certain we can arrange for changes of scenery throughout the day so you need not fret."

"I am not fretting," he retorted.

She brought her face down to his level. Goodness she was lovely especially when she was angry. Her amber eyes took on a deeper hue and nearly flashed fire at him. "You most certainly are fretting and hurt and angry, which you are entitled to be, but do not give up yet." She stood up straight and put her hands on her hips. "Will there be anything else for now?"

"You are not my servant," he growled. She turned to walk towards the door.

"We will see about that. I am certainly not leaving now." She shut the

35

ELIZABETH JOHNS

door quickly behind her before he could reply. He certainly could not go after her and argue, but he needed to think. He did not want her out alone again, and she was certainly stubborn enough that she would not take his money now that she had said as much. At least she was here for now and that was one thing less for him to worry about. He would let her think she was the deuced housekeeper until he was well enough to argue as her equal and convince her otherwise. Besides, it just felt right having her here again. He had been hurt by her defection to Peter, but had spent years pretending he was happy for them—trying to behave as though nothing had changed. If only he had stood up to his father. Instead, he had purchased a commission and followed Peter and Kitty to Spain.

He cursed. Lying in bed for another month was going to kill him. He had never been able to sit still and despite the pain, he longed to move about. Perhaps Kitty was right that he could be moved. He wondered if he could use crutches, as he had seen some of the amputees using. For now, he swallowed the contents of his glass in one long drink, hoping that it would dull his pain and numb his thoughts and that he would wake up after the bone had healed.

~

CARING for Matthias in a sisterly way again would be one of the hardest things Kitty had ever done. She had never stopped loving him, but had done her best to leave those feelings behind when she'd married Peter. The old Earl had been correct that she had cherished dreams of wedding Matthias. She had thought he reciprocated her feelings. She had been wrong, but no matter, he needed her now and she needed him, although in an entirely different way. And now her eyes were open to the harsh realities of life. The past was the past and they had to move on with their lives. They were family, after all. Her actions needed to concentrate on helping him heal and distracting him from his inability to move. As children, he had never been able to sit still for long.

She went to fetch a bonnet and pelisse, determined to do something good for Matthias. When she went to the stables to ask for a trap or gig to drive herself to the village, an argument ensued. Unless his lordship gave permission, she would be driven by a groom. Kitty sensed a long struggle ahead of her to convince the servants she was one of them. The head groom, Swann, (she could not think of anyone less aptly named), remembered her and politely reminded her she had been brought up a lady right there in that house. There was no objection to her driving the gig, he went on, but it was more than he dared to let her go without protection.

One battle at a time, so to speak, she told herself. As long as she was allowed to stay and go to the village without having to walk, she would not press her luck.

It was a perfect summer morning, the dew still not fully evaporated. The lush green carpet of vegetation and fully leafed trees emitted a fragrance that was eminently summer. Bluebells and daisies blanketed the meadow beside the road as they left the gates of the Close and turned towards the village. It had been so long—close to five years now? Would anyone recognize her here? A lot can change in five years, but she doubted the entire village had left or passed away in that time.

After a drive of perhaps a mile and a half, the gig pulled into the quintessential English Village, as Kitty had come to think of it after the years on the Peninsula where stucco and tile roofs were more common. She revelled in the familiar thatched roofs and white stone of her youth, still surrounded by ivy and the bright blooms of summer.

The butcher and the baker were on the left-hand side, the blacksmith and village shop on the other. The church's spire could be seen further down the high street beyond the White Horse Tavern and Inn. A rush of emotions swept over her, much like when she had stood at the gates of Thackeray Close, but for some reason she had had less doubt of her acceptance there. Certainly, everyone had known of her marriage to Peter and everyone would know of his death as a military hero.

"You may set me down here, Thomas," she said to the young footman who had not quite grown into his height as they neared the inn. She suspected he would enjoy spending his time there, waiting for her. "I will return here when I have finished my errand."

"Yes, ma'am," he answered, tipping his hat to her.

She decided her best form of attack would be to call at the rectory. She knew that Mr. Henderson had called since Matthias's return, but without knowing her status, Kitty had kept her presence quiet. Now that Matthias knew she was there and would not make her leave—at least for the nonce—she would no longer remain hidden.

She lifted the knocker on the door and let it drop, remembering the afternoons she had spent here with Peter and Matthias. They had been receiving tutoring in Latin and she had been allowed to tag along. Kitty discovered she had acquired more knowledge than she would have imagined while on the Peninsula. It came in very handy, when having to learn to speak Spanish.

It seemed so long ago... the familiar smells of baking and old leather-bound books reached her through the windows. The door opened to an elderly housekeeper.

"Mrs. Jones?" Kitty asked, pleased to see a familiar face.

The woman looked at her carefully then recognition crossed her face. "Miss Kitty? I mean, Mrs. Gordon?"

"It is I. Is Mr. or Mrs. Henderson in?"

"The missus is. The Rector be out making calls. Come on in to the drawing room and I will let her know you're here."

"Thank you," Kitty said as she was shown into the room. Nothing seemed to have changed except for some fading and wear. The Turkish carpet, with its geometric shapes and bold hues of red, dark blue and gold, was still the same, if less vibrant. She had spent hours trying to count them and determine what the strange shapes were when she was a child, on the occasions she had come with the Countess to sewing groups for the parish poor.

"Kitty?" an elderly voice asked from the doorway.

"Mrs. Henderson." Kitty walked over with her hands outstretched to greet the gentlewoman. Something was different besides her now grey hair and wrinkled face. She was straining to see. Kitty grasped her hands and squeezed.

"Forgive me, my sight is failing. I am so pleased you have returned home."

Home. There was that strange, almost foreign word again.

"Please be seated. Mrs. Jones is bringing tea."

Once they were seated on a sofa with their tea, Kitty was unsure where to begin.

Fortunately, Mrs. Henderson spoke first. "We all thought you would return when poor Peter died."

"I did briefly," Kitty confessed. It was going to be difficult not to besmirch Sir Nigel's name, but he was in part responsible for her present circumstances.

"Oh," was all Mrs. Henderson said as she sipped her tea.

"I have been in London trying to make my way," Kitty explained cautiously. "But now I have returned to take over as housekeeper for his lordship. Mrs. Harlow wishes to retire and live with her sister."

Mrs. Henderson frowned, but did not speak condemning words. "And how is his lordship?"

Kitty knew whatever words she uttered next would be repeated to the entire village. "He has recovered from a fever, but it appears his leg is broken. That is partially why I have come. Is old Mr. Bailey still crafting items from wood? I was hoping to have a crutch made for his lordship. I saw some of the amputees with such things and it enabled them to be mobile."

When Kitty was a child, Mr. Bailey would carve the most intricate nativity sets. She had always been fascinated by them.

Mrs. Henderson shook her head. "He passed away over a year ago, but his son might be able to help... though you might have to send to London for something."

Kitty had been afraid of that.

Mrs. Henderson finished her tea and sought for the saucer with her fingers, placing the cup back carefully. "Does Sir Nigel know you're to be a servant at the Close?"

"It is not my concern if he does or not," Kitty answered frankly.

"There will be talk," she warned. "I am surprised his lordship is allowing it."

Kitty hesitated. "Mrs. Harlow has not yet left."

"Ah," the lady said with understanding.

"I am a widow and must make my own way now. I hope I may rely on you to reassure anyone who may show concern that this is my idea not his lordship's. Nevertheless, he will be in need of a housekeeper soon and I am in need of a position."

Kitty rose to leave, having come to the end of her half-hour. In the general way of things, housekeepers did not make calls on ladies, but sometimes allowances could be made in small villages. Kitty knew it was a strange situation for everyone.

Mrs. Henderson stood up and looked at Kitty with pity, whether or not she realized she was doing it. "I think it is a shame if Sir Nigel did not ensure that you were taken care of, but I will do my best to see there is no talk. I believe people will understand because they know you."

It was the best Kitty could hope for. She dipped a curtsy, hoping Mrs. Henderson could see it, and took her leave, heading for the young Mr. Bailey and hoping he could help with what she needed.

CHAPTER 5

*M*atthias was not going to allow something as trivial as a broken leg keep him from walking again. Now if he could only convince said limb to cooperate. It had helped having the leg splinted, but he still broke out in a cold sweat any time he became vertical—even when holding on to the arms of a chair.

It seemed likely that something besides his bone had been damaged, but he would not dwell on that now. He could not. He stood again, and counted to ten as the shock to his body lessened with harsh breaths. If he did this enough times, surely his body would grow accustomed? He knew part of the problem was weakness from being ill for so long. Nine…ten. He collapsed back into the chair and tried to recover. A knock on the door then interrupted his sorry imitation of exercise.

"Enter."

The door opened and Hornsby brought in a tray. He eyed Matthias suspiciously.

"What have you been doing, my lord?"

"That is none of your concern," he snapped.

The batman grumbled under his breath as he brought in the tray of food and arranged it before Matthias on a small table.

41

Kidney pie, bacon, eggs and toast. If he did not start moving soon, he would be fatter than the pigs in the sties.

"Is there anything else, my lord?"

"Yes. I would like to go outside this afternoon."

The batman frowned, but did not argue. "Very well, sir. I will come back to take you out after you have partaken of your meal."

Matthias still had a voracious appetite. *I'm making up for over a month without food,* he justified to himself. He was not fat yet, at least, but still much weaker than he would like.

When Hornsby returned, he was determined to assist in his transportation outdoors.

Hornsby had brought two footmen with him. "I do not wish to be carried, Hornsby," Matthias said.

The batman's eyes narrowed. "Dr. Beverly said you were not to put weight on that leg for weeks."

"I heard the man," he bit out savagely. "However, if I lean on you, I still have one good leg. The same as I have been hobbling on out of my chamber."

Hornsby was shaking his head.

"Thomas and David may follow."

"Mrs. Gordon will beat the daylights out of me."

"You are more afraid of her than you are of me?" Matthias asked with disbelief. It had been her suggestion!

"The first role of being a servant in any house is to keep the ladies happy," Hornsby explained. "Besides, she ain't too good to dirty her hands."

"She should never have had to," Matthias retorted bitterly, wondering how he had lost control over his own household. Too many servants would see work as a fault in a lady, but Hornsby had known Kitty in the Peninsula, and it was a different matter entirely. Matthias wanted to know what she had been doing for the past several days, but he was afraid to ask. She had not visited him again.

"How has she been fitting in?" he grumbled as he took a quick swig of brandy before trying to move again.

Hornsby narrowed his eyes at the spirits, the impertinent rogue, but Matthias knew he understood.

"Mrs. Harlow is allowing her to perform a few of her usual duties, but she is not pleased about it."

"Is she making her displeasure obvious?"

"I have witnessed little of their converse, but of course, there is talk among the lesser servants." He sniffed, as if such behaviour were beneath him.

"Make it stop." As though Hornsby had the power to do so, Matthias reflected ruefully. Still...

The batman shook his head and removed the tray and table out of the way.

Matthias put his arms on the sides of the chair and hefted himself upright. Eyes closed, he waited for the wave of nausea to pass and then held out an arm for Hornsby. They—he—hopped and hobbled through the door out to the landing above the stairs. He could not do it. That short jaunt had left him feeling as though he had been pummelled in ten rounds by Gentleman Jackson himself.

He stopped to catch his breath, but knew he was beaten.

Hornsby waited for his order. "My lord?"

"I cannot."

"Well, I would not have reckoned you could come this far, so that's something innit?"

A grunt of annoyance was all the answer he could give the valet.

"Thomas, David and I will put you in a chair and carry you down the stairs. Why not let us?"

Thomas stepped forward with the offending object to prove Hornsby's point.

Matthias grabbed the railing and looked to the ceiling. He wanted to bellow with frustration.

"You cannot expect to make a recovery overnight," *her* voice said coolly from behind him.

"And why not?" he growled. Something about her made him angry. Was it because she reminded him of everything he had lost? Was it her calm? It was hardly fair, but he could not seem to help himself.

43

"I assume that is a rhetorical question or shall I attempt to explain basic laws of nature and make us both sound like fools?"

"Come here. I do not like you speaking to my back."

She stepped forward and looked surprisingly shy for the tartness of her voice a moment ago. She had fully outfitted herself in house-keeper's garb from the dark worsted wool with a freshly starched white apron, to the plain white cap on her head. He hated it.

"Take it off," he commanded as though she were one of his sergeants.

She crossed her arms in front of her and narrowed her gaze.

"This attire is appropriate for my position."

He scowled. "I did not agree to that."

He saw the look of uncertainty in her eyes and felt like a scoundrel —until she raised her chin in the air. "Very well. I will be changed before you return from your outing."

"I am not going on an outing," he retorted.

"Coward," she muttered before turning away.

He felt Hornsby's hand stiffen on his arm.

"No," he said, suddenly calm.

"Then prove it," she said, already halfway down the hall.

"If you take off the cap and apron." What had he just committed himself to? And why was he arguing with her as if they were children again?

He watched her turn back and glare at him as she untied the apron then the cap. She dropped them on the nearby table without ever removing her eyes from him. It was a clear challenge.

He gave a reluctant nod and David and Thomas brought the chair forward. He sat back down into it, trying to keep the relief he felt from his face, less Kitty think she had won. Well, perhaps she had bested him by a small margin in this battle, but he would win the war.

The chair lifted beneath him and tipped back as he was carried down the stairs—every single one jarring his leg with pain as excruci-ating as he imagined an axe to his leg would be. They carried him on out towards the lake and as soon as the sun and fresh air hit his face, some of his black mood fell away.

They set him down beneath the shade of a tree, then stood at attention, as if waiting his next command.

"Leave me," he said deliberately trying to keep his voice neutral. He was angry, yes, but not with them. They doubtless felt as though they had just moved a boulder up and down a mountain.

As the servants bowed and walked away, Matthias could not help but recall the scenes of his life that had been played out here. Every afternoon he, Kitty and Peter had played in this very spot or nearby, sometimes with his brother too, though they were several years his junior. The old swing hung from the large branch on the massive willow tree at the lake's edge, its rope now frayed and the wooden swing looking its age. How tempted he was to try to hop on and throw himself into the water! He barked a harsh noise that might have resembled a laugh. In his condition he would probably sink straight to the bottom. The thought was more alluring than it should be.

"Stop it!" he commanded himself. Self-pity was the worst of sins, he knew. It did not make him feel any better. If his younger brother was a worthy fellow, he might not feel obliged to keep himself alive. However, Henry had been his justification. The reason he had defied his father and bought his commission. Yet how would he go on if this was a glimpse into his future? That was a sobering thought, causing him to take the flask from his pocket and draw heavily on the liquid fire that reminded him he was not dead...yet.

⁓

KITTY WATCHED the scene unfold from a distance. Things were worse than she had thought. Matthias had changed—understandably—but was he the same person she had always loved, still, beneath this new veneer? Would he ever come back to her?

It was a fine line she would have to walk. Clearly he did not wish for her to be his servant, yet it seemed unlikely there would ever be any more. She thought she had accepted that when she had married Peter.

Her mind raced furiously. How could she convince Matthias to let her stay? It would be difficult, and no matter whether she was there as a relation or as a housekeeper, some people would talk. There was no one she could call upon to act as a chaperone and besides, it was rather too late in the day for that nicety, even though he was virtually incapacitated.

Stones splashed with a plunk as he threw them in anger. He had always been an expert at skimming them, yet since he was not at the proper angle he had, apparently, settled for throwing them. Mayhap it would release some of his frustration. She refused to believe this was the new Matthias. Once he healed from his injury he would walk again and his spirits would improve, surely. But she also knew there was no guarantee and that she could not leave him.

She watched him take a long drink from a flask and shook her head. "That will never do," she muttered to herself. There had to be something in Lady Thackeray's garden that could help him. If only she knew what... but was he drinking to help the pain or to try to forget? There was no remedy for that.

First though, she needed to address the problem of him accepting her in this new role. Kitty pursed her lips. It would take convincing Mrs. Harlow to leave, she believed, yet the devoted servant would not go without Matthias's blessing.

Kitty steeled herself for the confrontation and started down the path that descended the hill to the lake.

"Intending to shed your clothes and jump in? I am afraid I will have to watch instead of joining you," he said as she drew near, without once looking away from the water.

"There is no need to be crude," she scolded. "I came to speak with you, if you must know."

"Not, I trust, to feed me false hope and pity. I have had large doses of that ad nauseum."

"I think I know you better than to offer you falsehoods."

"Just so. Then what do you want?"

"I want you to send Mrs. Harlow away. She was hoping to retire when you returned."

"Then she may go with my blessing. But you will not replace her."

"I have never known you to be cruel, Matthias." Hurtful, but not deliberately cruel. It had to be the drink making him this way.

"People change. You, of all people, should understand that. They change and they disappoint you." There was so much history behind those sentences, she thought.

"That is an understatement," she snapped and indignantly turned away, beginning to stride back to the house. He needed her, why could he not see that?

"Kitty!" he called.

She stopped but did not turn around. "You know I cannot stay here otherwise," she protested.

"Then leave. I will see you have what you need."

"I cannot be kept by you, can you not see that?"

"Only if you care for the opinion of others. What is the difference in your being here or somewhere else? I have several relatives who have no compunction whatsoever in accepting my funds."

"You know very well why," she grumbled. Was he so cruel that he would make her say the words aloud?

His tone softened a little. "And do you think, by wearing that ugly uniform, it will make people talk less?"

"It will at least give me justification."

"I do not want you as my housekeeper, Kitty." He took another draw on his drink.

"Why are you being so stubborn? You need someone and I need a position, Matthias." She could hear the pleading and desperation in her voice. The thought of going back on her own and leaving him like this was unbearable.

"Temptation." The word was slurred.

She turned around and he was watching her.

"I beg your pardon?" Had she heard him correctly? He would never speak to her like this sober.

He barked a laugh. "You had better give me a wide berth, then," he warned. "I cannot vouch for my actions."

Matthias had always been the most honourable man she had ever known. "I am not afraid of you."

"You should be. War changes people. Neither of us are the same as we were five years ago."

"No, indeed. But your character doesn't change," she argued. "Or are you going to allow spirits to turn you into a monster?"

"Shall I shoot your leg and horse out from under you? How would you feel, having watched two of your best friends fall right before your eyes?"

She winced at the reminder as though it were a physical blow. Tears were streaming down her face before she could tell herself not to react. She turned and ran, ignoring him when he called after her. He had gone too far and he knew it, but he could not come after her, could he?

Perhaps returning here had been a mistake. She had had her doubts and that was why it had taken her two years and destitution to make the decision. But would it be bearable to see Matthias like this? She could not allow him to ruin himself in such a way. She ran all the way to the old stone bridge and leaned over the edge, her sides burning with pain and her breaths stertorous.

Watching the sun gleaming on the rocks and the water trickle by helped her to calm and her breathing to slow. A decision had to be made. She either stayed to help Matthias and face the consequences, or she left and ended back on the streets, starving. Neither was appealing.

She let all of the tears fall: the ones for what the three of them had used to be; the ones for Peter's death and their short marriage; and the ones for the friendship that they had pledged would be eternal. She owed it to Matthias to help him, whether he fully healed or not.

The sun was beginning to fall in the sky by the time she returned to the house, but instead of going inside, she found her way to the herb garden. She wound her way through the familiar plants and flowers, pleased she could still recognize the three she had put to memory. There had to be something here that could help him. But would he accept her help? She still didn't know what he meant by all of his words.

He had never before spoken to her thus; in fact, he had always been there to support her, especially once Lady Thackeray had died and Lord Thackeray had decided to turn against her. Matthias had always been her champion...until now.

If nothing else, she owed it to him to support him through his recovery and ensure he did not drink himself to death.

"Miss Kitty?"

Kitty started, looking up from the daisy she held, the petals of which she had completely plucked off.

"Mrs. Harlow. Is something amiss?" Thoughts flashed through her mind of Matthias throwing himself into the lake and being unable to swim.

"I was worried about you. You have been gone for hours."

Kitty nodded. "His lordship and I argued."

"Was it about me? Because he told me I could leave." She worried her apron.

"Good. I am happy for you. You deserve a peaceful retirement." She did not wish to reveal any more of their argument. It would not make her leave. Kitty would be much busier with the housekeeper gone and the task of helping Matthias would be easier.

CHAPTER 6

*H*e was a blackguard. Matthias thumped his fist on the arm of the chair. No matter how frustrated he was, he should not take it out on Kitty. She had lost her husband and friend and he had been cruel. No gentleman would ever mention what happened on the battlefield.

Leaning his head back over his chair, he stared up at the leaves blowing in the soft breeze overhead, hanging from the branches they had been used to climb as children.

But they were children no more.

Why was she being so difficult? He could easily provide for her elsewhere—somewhere she could be happy and comfortable. Of a certainty, staying there with him would not be comfortable.

Did she not realize how he felt about her—how it had been torture to see her marry their best friend?

He groaned. If he did not agree to her scheme, she was obstinate enough to leave with nowhere to go. Curse her stubbornness! He wanted to drown himself in pity. He would have to let her stay, but he did not have to like it. Perhaps if he pensioned off Mrs. Harlow, then Kitty would be too busy to cause him undue bother.

That decision made, he tried to allow himself to sleep but his leg throbbed in tempo with his heartbeat. If she objected to him drinking, what did she expect him to do instead? He took a small sip from his flask—much smaller than he wished for. That should at least make her happy. He was able to drift into a fitful sleep, but even there he could not escape the memory of Kitty.

"My lord?"

He felt the tap on his shoulder. "My lord?"

Matthias opened one of his eyes to see Hornsby leaning over him. "There is no need to hover!"

The batman grunted. "I thought you were dead, there, for a moment. You've never been hard to wake up before."

"I am awake now. What is it you want?"

"It is time to go back to the house, sir. Cook has made your favourite minced pie."

"I cannot stomach food now. I am tired of sitting in this spot, though."

Hornsby bent over and picked him up.

"Now I am to suffer this indignity as well," he grumbled. Although, he reflected sourly, Hornsby was as strong as an ox. He could bear the weight.

"Where to, my lord?" Hornsby asked as the front door opened for them.

"My study. And send Mrs. Harlow to me."

Hornsby deposited him on the sofa in the study. It had been his father's sanctum, but Matthias had worked hard to put his own stamp on it. His relationship with his father had deteriorated after what he had done to Kitty, and Matthias had never quite forgiven him for it.

It was partly why Matthias had not been able to bring himself to marry, especially not the ladies his father had chosen for him. His father had died while he had been absent with the army the first time, and Matthias wondered if his sire had regretted sending Kitty away and then issuing ultimatums to his heir.

He blew out his breath. It would be necessary to tread carefully with Kitty as well, lest he repeat his father's mistakes. He did not wish to lose her again, even if she had chosen Peter and the knowledge still stung. It was irrational, he knew, when he had not offered for her himself, but she had not trusted him enough to wait.

Somehow it felt as though he was stuck in a deep crevasse with slippery walls and no way out. Things were not so desperate, he attempted to reason with himself, but they felt desperate. He felt helpless.

"You wanted to see me, my lord?" Mrs. Harlow stood before him. Very likely she had knocked and he had not heard.

"Yes. Please have a seat so I do not have to look up at you."

Reluctantly, she sat down but stayed on the edge of her chair.

"Miss Kitty has told me you wish to retire."

"Only when you are ready for me to do so, my lord. I would never leave you in your time of need," she sputtered, as if offended by the suggestion.

"You have been training Miss Kitty, I understand, and she undeniably knows the house well."

"That she does," the housekeeper hesitantly agreed.

"But?"

"It is not my place to say, my lord."

"You have known both of us since infancy. I give you leave to speak."

"Very well. I think she will manage the household well enough, but she was not brought up to be a servant. She is a gentlewoman, my lord."

"She will not accept my help in any other way, Mrs. Harlow. What am I to do?"

"That is why I agreed to go along with the charade. You should have seen her when she arrived. She looked a sight, my lord." Her voice cracked, choking with emotion at the remembrance.

Matthias had not known *that*. Guilt shot through him, sharper than any bullet wound had. "And she is stubborn enough to go back to that rather than take a penny from me."

"Sir Nigel should be ashamed of himself," she spat.

"I will deal with him in time," Matthias vowed.

"People will talk no matter what because of the history, if you will pardon my saying so. I fear Sir Nigel will try to turn everyone hereabouts against her if there is any suggestion of his being at fault."

"How Nigel and Peter came from the same stock, I will never know." People probably said that about Matthias and his brother, he thought dourly. "Either way, you should assume your well-deserved retirement, with a suitable pension of course. Kitty will step into a well-run house and only needs to maintain the standards you have instituted. You are to join your sister, I believe?" He thought he had overheard that somewhere.

"Yes, my lord. We have purchased a cottage by the sea in Exeter."

"Perhaps, one day, we shall meet again. My mother always tried to maintain a connexion with long-serving retainers. I will request Miss Kitty to do so, if you will furnish her with your new direction. Your accounts should be in order. And if you ever need anything—" He found his throat constricting and was forced to swallow. Another principal person in his life was leaving him. It somehow made keeping Kitty here more necessary. He hated goodbyes. He reached out his hand. "Forgive me for not standing properly. I wish you well, Mrs. Harlow."

She nodded as she dabbed a handkerchief to her eyes, then blew her nose. She rose and curtsied deeply before leaving the room.

Selfishly, he wanted her to stay. She had always been there and was as much a part of Thackeray Close as the house itself.

"My lord?" Hayes interrupted the maudlin mood about to descend. "There is a Mr. Bailey here. He says he has a delivery for you."

"I suppose you had better show him in, then."

"My lord." The young, but large man bowed before him.

"Forgive me. I am somewhat indisposed, as you can see."

"'Tis why I am here. I came to see Mrs. Gordon, but as no one seems to know where she is, I thought... She commissioned this for you, my lord."

Matthias was disturbed by two things. One, where was Kitty? And two, she had commissioned something for him?

The man unwrapped his parcel and stood it before Matthias. "Is that a crutch?" Matthias had seen some of the disabled veterans using such things before. Had he not just been thinking he could use one?

"Yes, my lord. Miss Kitty drew a sketch of it and afforded me with your measurements. Said she had seen such on the Continent, used by some of the injured men. She thought as how maybe it would help you get about whilst you recover."

Matthias took the piece of polished wood and fingered it gently, despite it being strong enough to bear a grown man's weight. This was about shoulder high and had a special bar for his hand to hold on. He did not know whether to be touched by her thoughtfulness or crack it over something in frustration for his situation.

"Do you do you know how to use it, my lord?"

"I suppose I do. I have also seen what she speaks of."

"Very good, then. If you have any further need, please do not hesitate to contact me." The man put a small card on the great mahogany library table, bowed and left.

Matthias watched the door close behind the man and was filled with curiosity and a tinge of hope. Would he be able to get about, even now, with this contraption?

He pulled his way forward to the edge of the sofa, pain shooting through his leg with any contraction of it. Once vertical, however, he would not be required to move it.

He used the arms of the chair to push himself up and broke out into a cold sweat from that movement alone. Standing for a moment, he tried to catch his breath, and then reached for the crutch. Having positioned it on his arm, he thought about the movement. Slowly, he took one step forward...and collapsed into a heap on the floor, cursing his clumsiness.

"What the devil are you doing?" Hornsby asked as he burst into the room, the tray in his hands at a precarious angle.

"I think I need a second crutch," Matthias said, looking up sheepishly.

54

~

WHEN KITTY finally felt sufficiently composed to return to the house, Hornsby sought her out and explained what had happened during her absence.

"I left his lordship in the study long enough to fetch him a tray. While I was gone, Mr. Bailey delivered the crutch you ordered. That was a very kind gesture, Mrs. Gordon."

Kitty could feel her cheeks warm under the praise. "I wish only for him to be back on his feet as soon as may be. You know well how difficult it is for him to be idle."

"That I do, ma'am. But I thought you should know, that as I was returning with his tray, I heard a heavy thud, and when I opened the door, I found him huddled on the floor."

"Oh, good gracious!" she exclaimed. "Is he harmed?"

"No," the batman replied, "thankfully not. He was laughing at his clumsiness but he does think he could use a second crutch so as to balance the weight."

"Oh, of course. I had not considered that. I had the intention of going to the village in the morning, so I will call upon Mr. Bailey and ask him to make another."

"I thank you, ma'am." Bowing, the manservant turned to leave. Kitty stopped him.

"Hornsby, do you think his lordship would try some herbal remedies if I prepared them? Or would I be on a fool's errand?"

"I think, ma'am, that if anyone could persuade him to take them, that person is you."

Kitty gave a nod. "Will you please try to see that he does not receive too many spirits?"

Hornsby hesitated. "That will be somewhat more difficult, ma'am. Most of the servants will do as he asks, of course."

"Then, as the new housekeeper, I will speak to the butler. I refuse to allow him to drink himself to death."

"I fear, if his lordship commands, not even Mr. Hayes may gainsay him. Nevertheless, I will do my best to help."

Early the following morning, there were tearful goodbyes as Mrs. Harlow took her leave.

"Take good care of him and write if it isn't too inconvenient," the elder woman said. "I still think it is a shame you aren't the lady of the house, but I know you'll do your best by him."

"I will," Kitty said, trying not to cry as Mrs. Harlow climbed in to the travelling coach.

After waving her on her way, Kitty hurried down to the servants' hall for breakfast. She had to start as she meant to go on. The others were already seated and at once there was an almost deafening sound of chairs being pushed back as everyone rose to their feet.

"Good morning, Mr. Hayes, everyone. As you know, I will be taking over Mrs. Harlow's duties. I will have a hard task to follow in her footsteps, and her retirement is well earned. Everything is running very smoothly, thanks to your hard work, and I do not see any reason to make changes when things are working. Please attend to your duties as before and if I can be of help, please ask."

She saw looks of wariness exchanged among some of the older servants, while some of the younger ones nodded their heads.

Kitty continued, "I am sure we all want the same things—a pleasant place to work and live, and to see his lordship recover. I intend to spend a good deal of my time working in the herb garden and still-room, not hovering over you. You all know what to do." She prayed they would be receptive to her approach. She knew she was taking a risk.

Hornsby moved to stand before her and raised his cup of tea. "Welcome, Mrs. Gordon." The others followed suit whether they approved of her or not.

"Thank you," she said as she took her seat at the foot of the table. It was clear they were uncomfortable with her presence in the hall, as they were quiet and averted eye contact, but she picked up her fork and ate as though she had been a servant all her life. Certainly she was eating better than she had much of her time as a lady on her own. When the meal ended, she excused herself and set off to the village, the grooms still not allowing her to take the trap herself. One battle at a time, she told herself.

Her first stop was at Mr. Bailey's joinery workshop, and then she made her way to the village apothecary. Despite having been resident at the Close for a couple of months, now, she still felt some stares and noticed whispers wherever she walked about. In the beginning, she had expected people would wonder who she was and then speculate about why she had returned, but by now, she mused, her presence should have been accepted. As the old Earl's ward, she had always been treated as a lady, but when she saw the squire's wife, Mrs. Gillespie, pointedly turn and cross the street rather than greet her, Kitty knew something was wrong.

As she turned into the apothecary's small shop, she hoped Mr. Satterlee would be either unaware of the gossip or not care. He had been on friendly terms with Lady Thackeray due to their shared passion for herbalism.

"How may I help you?" he asked with a friendly smile. He had aged a great deal. "Is that you, Miss Kitty?"

"It is I, Mr. Satterlee. I did not know if you would remember me." Being in the shop, filled with the scents of plants, and shelves and shelves of medicinal jars, brought back a flood of memories.

"Oh, yes, you used always to be by her ladyship's side," he said, with fondness and a hint of sadness. "How may I be of help?"

"You may have heard that his lordship was wounded in battle."

"Yes, I had heard he was shot. How is he?"

"Well... but not. He took a bullet into the bone, and while he has recovered from the infection, he still cannot bear weight. I came to ask what you would recommend for the knitting of bone, and also pain. He will not take laudanum."

"I cannot blame him for that, though sometimes it is necessary." He scratched his head and adjusted his spectacles.

"Yes, but he chooses spirits instead. So far, he has had only a little, but I fear if there is not an alternative, he might drown himself in them."

He nodded, understanding. "There are a few things you may try. I suspect, unless the garden is overrun, that the Close should have a supply of most."

He turned to sort through his jars and drawers before facing her again. He spread some of the leaves on the table. "This is Comfrey, known as boneset, and this is what it should look like after you harvest it and dry it. Ointment can be made from the roots, but fresh leaves can be bruised and put directly on the wound and then gently bandaged. For a poultice, boil a good handful of chopped leaves wrapped in cotton, cool and wring out the excess water and apply. Care must be taken when plants are not in flower though, as the leaves are similar to those of foxgloves, which can be lethal." Then he took a key and opened a small chest very carefully, gently pulling a sachet from inside.

"This, however, you will not find in any garden in England."

"What is it?" she asked, burning with curiosity.

"It is a herb grown in India. Its healing properties are reported to be miraculous." He chuckled, as if he strongly doubted such a thing existed.

"His lordship could certainly benefit from a miracle at the moment."

"I have a friend who works for the East India Company and is able to procure it for me. It is commonly known as Asthisamhari and is a succulent of the family *Vitaceae*."

That was far beyond Kitty's limited knowledge of herbs. "How does it work?"

"As to that, I could not say. Unfortunately, some parts of medicine are still in their infancy. However, you can make a paste and apply topically. It can also be taken internally, though it is very bitter. It is said to help with knitting of the bone."

"I hope his lordship will agree to it. If not, I will have to be devious."

The old man chuckled. "If only all of my patients had a champion such as you."

Kitty opened her purse, suspecting this herb would be very dear. But it would be worth it. She paid Mr. Satterlee and then wrapped up her purchases in her reticule. As she exited his shop, she almost ran into someone who was walking past the doorway.

"I beg your pardon," she said quickly before looking up—and finding she was face to face with Sir Nigel Gordon, Peter's elder brother. The dark eyes that had been full of laughter and mischief in the younger brother were sanctimonious and judgemental in the elder one.

He sucked in his breath when he recognized her.

"Sir Nigel," she said, trying not to sound bitter.

He puffed out his chest. "Is it true?"

"Is what true?" Kitty had no idea what he was talking about.

"The words are too distasteful to say. Yet someone must preserve our good name."

"Whatever are you referring to, Gordon?"

"It is said that you are living at the Close as his *mistress*." He emphasized the last word with all the righteous indignation he could probably muster, spittle forming on his lips with the last syllable.

Kitty had known that such rumours were a possibility, but they hurt nonetheless.

"He will never marry you, you know. He would not marry you then, so why would he now? Especially if you are giving him what he wants without the bonds of holy matrimony." Sir Nigel sneered. "I must insist you leave there at once to preserve my family's good name —which, unfortunately, you share."

"Your good name?" She barely contained her fury. "You had the chance to help me and you offered me a pittance and no shelter. You do not support me, therefore you do not have the right to tell me what I may or may not do!"

"You blacken the family name by your actions!"

Kitty gasped at his insolence. "Your heart is as black as your hair!" She turned her back on him and walked away, her heart pounding and her face burning. She hated confrontation and he always brought out the worst in her. She was mortified and knew she would regret her rash tongue. Of a certainty he would make her suffer for it.

"Do you deny it?" he called after her, his tone demanding and harsh.

She neither turned nor deigned to answer such an insult. It was not only an insult to herself but also to Lord Thackeray.

She held her head up as she brushed through the growing number of spectators who had come out of their houses to see what the disturbance was. Kitty had not known she could feel such utter humiliation.

CHAPTER 7

*M*atthias's head was pounding like the devil. He groaned and rolled over as much as he could on to his side, pulling his pillow up over his head. *Pound! Pound! Pound!* He then realized it was not solely his head, although that definitely was pounding, but someone at the front door.

Blessedly, someone answered the door, but it was not long until he heard footsteps climbing the stairs. He groaned, then cursed. Mayhap the intruder would not be for him.

"My lord?" Hayes asked tentatively after knocking and opening the door.

"Tell them to go away," he grumbled.

"I do not think that will be possible, sir."

"At least tell them to come back at a reasonable hour," Matthias commanded tartly.

The butler coughed discreetly as butlers do. "It is half after two in the afternoon, my lord."

"Who is this beastly guest to demand an audience in such a rude manner?"

"Sir Nigel Gordon, my lord."

Matthias sat up straight in anger and immediately winced. His head was throbbing almost as much as his leg. "The devil!" he cursed.

"Shall I send Hornsby to you?"

"If you must."

"Very good, my lord."

Matthias leaned his head back on the headboard. Nothing good ever came from a visit with Sir Nigel, even when he was in a good mood. Based on his infernal pounding, as if he were indeed trying to escape the fiery furnace, he was decidedly not in a good mood. Neither was Matthias.

He waited until Hornsby arrived with warm water.

"You took your time," Matthias remarked dryly, thinking at least twenty minutes had passed since Sir Nigel's arrival.

Hornsby scoffed in his familiar way. "It will do that pompous arse some good to cool his heels."

Matthias could not agree more. "Take your time in shaving me. I have no objection to making him wait, calling uninvited as he did."

"And you on your sickbed, sir. After the way he treated Mrs. Gordon, I have a mind to draw his cork."

"Has something new occurred?" Matthias asked, a bad feeling encroaching on his humour.

"Thomas said the turkey-cock humiliated her on the high street, in front of the whole village. Accused her of being your mistress, the dastard."

Matthias instantly wanted Sir Nigel's blood. "He is fortunate to find me incapacitated."

He was too angry to say another word as they finished his morning ablutions. His mind was fully occupied in pondering what to do.

"Where would you like to go, my lord?" Hornsby asked when Matthias was ready.

"I believe we should make a grand show of my incapacitation. That should set the stage nicely for his accusations. Will he dare say the words to my face when he sees my condition?"

"He deserves to be called out for such baseness. Anyone who knows Mrs. Gordon at all must know she would never behave thus."

"Just so." Certainly she would never do anything openly to sully Peter's name. What she might have done, while living on the streets, in order to survive... Matthias could barely contain his anger. Part of it was at himself for not personally ensuring Kitty had been properly taken care of.

Hornsby carried Matthias down the stairs and two footmen swung open the doors to the drawing room where Sir Nigel had, apparently, been pacing for over an hour.

"Thackeray!" he began and then stopped short when he saw Matthias being cradled like an infant in Hornsby's arms.

Matthias was not about to make this easy for Sir Nigel. As he was placed on the sofa he groaned, and only partially for dramatic effect.

"What may I do for you, Sir Nigel?" he asked in a pained voice as he adjusted his position.

"I am sorry for your injury," Sir Nigel said, sounding as if he were swallowing bile.

"Thank you. We do not know yet if it will mend—or, indeed, if I will walk again."

"Yes, well, I came to speak with you about my sister-in-law. I have been told she is living under your roof." He sniffed, an affectation Matthias could not stomach.

"Do tell me how it concerns you if she is? Did you not wash your hands of her with twenty pounds and—allow me the indulgence of plain speaking—a swift kick out of the door?"

Hornsby made a sound of approval in his throat and Matthias cast him a warning look. Hornsby had ever been one of those sergeants who spoke his mind. Had he worked for an unforgiving master, he would have been whipped constantly.

His comment eroded Sir Nigel's pretence of civility as Matthias had known it would.

"None of my concern?" he blustered. "She bears my name, man!"

Matthias remained outwardly calm, hoping it would only serve to infuriate Sir Nigel more. "Regrettable, I agree. However, she bears not your name but Peter's, God rest his soul. Your brother would have expected much more from you, you must know that. When Kitty swallowed her pride and asked you for help and a place to live, you washed your hands of her and from that moment she was no longer your responsibility."

"That's as may be, but now she has the audacity to flaunt herself in my village and take up residence under your roof. It is unforgivable! I will not tolerate it!"

"There is nothing for you to tolerate. She needed a home and she will always have one here. If you recall, she is also a distant relation of mine, and I take full responsibility for her welfare. You may go, in good conscience, knowing that you have rid yourself of her once and for all."

"That is not the way of such matters, and you know it! Rumours are already flying all over the village!" Sir Nigel argued.

"Rumours which, I daresay, you began! And what is more, you did not attempt to mitigate them but instead added fuel to the fire! I should call you out for insulting her so!"

Sir Nigel's face burned red and the veins throbbed in his neck. Could he be so kind as to have an apoplexy and save the world from his presence? Matthias suppressed his uncharitable wishes and returned his attention to the imbecile standing before him.

"As you can see, I am in no condition either to fight a duel or make anyone my mistress. I suggest you do your best to clear Kitty's good name—" He deliberately avoided using the name Gordon. "And allow her to proceed with her life. I returned from the war to find she's been grieving for Peter in abject poverty, no thanks to you. If ever I hear that you have uttered another word against her, then you will deal not only with me but very likely all of Peter's brethren in arms also, for they swore an oath to protect Kitty."

"If that is so, then where have they all been during her time of need?" Sir Nigel had the audacity to ask.

"They, sir, have been on the Continent, fighting against Napoleon, not sitting in their warm houses in England, withholding God-given blessings from widows in need. Now, if that will be all? Hayes, be so good as to show Sir Nigel out," Matthias ground out through a clenched jaw. He was ready to strangle the man.

"It would be my pleasure, my lord," Hayes replied as he ushered the pompous baronet through the drawing room door and then the heavy oaken portal of the front entrance.

Hornsby started clapping the moment they heard the front door shut with a thud. "Could a person be more blinded by self-right-eousness?"

"This will not be the end of it," Matthias predicted ominously.

"Very likely not," Hornsby agreed. "But at least in the village we servants can do our best to mitigate his insults. And given the way he was carrying on, you can bet the entire household is aware of his villainy by now and will support Mrs. Gordon."

Matthias nodded. "Do what you can."

"Would you like a tray, so you may break your fast?"

"Yes. If you would not mind helping me to the study. I should prefer to eat in there. And refill my flask while you are about it." He handed his man the silver flask, directing, not asking. He knew very well Kitty had told them to ration his spirits.

Now he needed to think. Something would have to be done, because he feared this was far from over. He knew from experience that Nigel did not play fair and would never accept that he was in the wrong.

Matthias had known from the first that Kitty's presence in his house would not be simple, and certainly the solution would not be either.

~

KITTY HAD TAKEN her time in returning to Thackeray Close. She had sent the groom back with the pony trap and walked, needing time to clear her head. She was burning with rage, deeply hurt and humili-ated; word of the quarrel would soon spread, and most likely she would be forced to leave. She had nowhere to go and it would be the hardest thing she had ever done to leave Matthias while he was injured. Whether he knew it or not, he needed her and she supposed she would have to endure the cruel words at least until he was better, because no one else was able to stand up to him.

With renewed determination, she stopped in the herb garden to find what Mr. Satterlee had recommended. While she was scouring the wide beds, she heard what she thought to be shouting coming from inside the house. She stopped and frowned, trying to listen through the open windows. Masculine voices were definitely raised. She crept towards the house, trying to discover what was happening without showing herself. Very well, she was eavesdropping.

"Yes, well, I came to speak with you about my sister-in-law. I have been told she is living under your roof."

"Do tell me how it concerns you if she is? Did you not wash your hands of her with twenty pounds and—allow me the indulgence of plain speaking—a swift kick out of the door?"

"Sir Nigel!" Kitty exclaimed under her breath. The audacity of the man! He must have come straight here, though she should not at all be surprised. Had he not confronted her on the main street of the village for all eyes and ears to see and hear?

She hurried closer to the house but stopped when she heard more of their conversation.

"If that is so, then where have they all been during her time of need?" Sir Nigel had the audacity to ask.

"They, sir, have been on the Continent fighting against Napoleon, not sitting in their warm houses in England withholding God-given blessings from widows in need. Now if that will be all? Hayes, be so good as to show so Nigel out."

. . .

"BRAVO, MATTHIAS." He was defending her. He had always despised Sir Nigel, so it was not shocking to hear him oppose the baronet, but it was touching nonetheless.

She leaned against the back of the house between two of the terrace doors, and waited for Sir Nigel to leave. A few minutes later she overheard Matthias ask Hornsby for more liquor and then request assistance to his study, which was the room on the other side of where she stood. She needed to speak with Matthias, to convince him to accept her help. Her heart quailed at the alternative but she lifted her chin and stiffened her spine. If he truly wanted her to leave, she would.

As she was about to step through the terrace doors, she heard Hornsby return.

"Oh, good man," Matthias said.

"Thomas brought your tray. Eat more than you drink, mind. The missus wouldn't be pleased."

"Mind your own business, Sergeant. 'Tis only to dull the pain. When my leg heals, I won't need it."

"As you say, my lord. Now, make certain you eat Cook's blackberry tarts. They are the best I've ever tasted."

"Cook is one of the jewels of the Close," Matthias agreed.

When it seemed as though Hornsby had left again, Kitty garnered her courage and stepped through the door.

"I was wondering when you would come in," Matthias said smugly.

"You knew I was out there?"

"Of course. You were never any good at hiding." He put a spoonful of tart into his mouth.

"I was not precisely hiding," she defended herself. "I was waiting. I wish to speak with you alone."

"Under the circumstances, I am not certain being alone is wise."

"I know, but how else are we to have a candid conversation?" she asked, growing exasperated.

"What did you wish to speak about?" He was going to toy with her and make her say it. He had always been thus.

"I thought we should address Sir Nigel's behaviour. You heard his accusations." That should suffice.

"He is a menace."

"You will hear no argument from me on that score, but many are saying the same in the village. If you want me to go, I will."

"Did you hear the entire conversation?" He looked up at her and fully met her gaze for the first time. Something shifted within her. It felt like their recent troubles had disappeared and a shadow of the old Matthias was looking at the old Kitty.

For a moment, she forgot to answer.

"Kitty?" he asked, a little furrow appearing between his brows.

"I—no, I do not believe I heard the entirety of the conversation, but I heard enough to know that you defended me and gave him a proper set down."

Matthias again looked at her strangely, as if five years of heartache, loss and war had not come between them. And Peter. He had definitely come between them. Her heart clenched at the thought of her husband and friend. She missed him terribly—and still struggled to forgive him for dying and leaving her alone.

"What are you thinking about?" Matthias interrupted.

"Peter."

"You still love him."

"How can you even say that, as if I would ever stop loving him? Of course I love him. I have always loved both of you. But what has that to do with the current predicament?"

He kept watching her in that way he had which made her feel very self-conscious, but she held her ground.

"I do not wish for you to leave."

She swallowed hard. "Do you mean that, truly? This is not based on your oath of honour or some misguided sense of pride?"

"Of course it is based on honour! I am surprised you could even ask."

"Yes, honour defines a gentleman. Someone should have told Sir Nigel that," she snapped. And turned to look out of the terrace doors.

"Judge me for myself alone. Kitty..." he began. She did not like the tone he used.

Turning, she met his gaze again and waited.

"There is a simple solution to all of this. It would stop the rumours and you would be secure for life."

She knew what was coming, and much though she had longed, at one time, to hear the words, they could not be borne like this. She shook her head but he said them anyway.

"We could marry, Kitty."

"Oh, Matthias, you know that is not a good idea."

"Why not?" He looked hurt. "We should have been wed all those years ago. You just said you loved me as you love Peter, and you married him."

That had been a mistake—a thousand times a mistake. Nevertheless, it did not take away her gratefulness to Peter, or the memories. She did not know how to respond.

"Kitty, do be reasonable about this. You might at least consider it."

Kitty had sworn that never again would she marry for the wrong reasons. Yet she had lost everything and would be a fool to turn down such an offer. To be married to Matthias for the wrong reasons would be pure agony every day. Being his housekeeper was preferable...at least until he took a wife... if they could have their friendship back. She shook her head again.

"I would rather be your housekeeper, if you can abide the gossip. I would rather have your friendship than have you come to hate me for binding you so."

Kitty waited for his response. He looked down at his tray and shuffled some food around on the plates. A brooding Matthias was distinctly uncomfortable. He had never been one to succumb to rage and took his time over thinking about what he would say next.

"If that is your wish, then so be it." He took his flask and appeared to empty the contents from it. Then he looked at her more coldly. "Now leave."

"Please do not be this way. You will drink yourself to death!"

"Who cares if I do? Lady Thackeray has the right to scold me, but a housekeeper does not."

Now he was going to be cruel. "Perhaps I should just go," she said flatly.

"If that is what you want. Whatever you do, I will see you are taken care of."

"Because of your honour?" she spat in anger. Despite the emboldening force of her ire, seconds afterwards she felt deflated. "I do not want to leave with matters between us like this." She slumped down on to the edge of the nearest chair and put her head in her hands. All she really wanted to do was cry herself to sleep and wake up with the whole situation having been a nightmare.

Matthias said nothing until she looked up again. "It seems we are at an impasse."

Already she could detect the effects of the spirits. She looked at the ceiling, trying to decide what to do. "May we make a bargain?"

"What do you propose?" A hint of amusement laced his question.

"I will stay and help you to heal while performing the duties of housekeeper…"

He snorted. "How the devil do you mean to help me heal?"

She cleared her throat. "Herbs. I have just been to the apothecary."

"My mother was very good with herbs. I remember her teaching you."

Kitty did not expound on the fact that she remembered little of what his mother had taught her. "So will you let me try?"

"That does not sound like much of a bargain. You would be doing all the work."

"There is a catch. You must cease drinking."

CHAPTER 8

*M*atthias should not have been surprised by her demands. "Do you guarantee you can control my pain?" he demanded, not wanting to make a bargain with the unknown. Better the devil he knew.

He saw from the look on Kitty's face that she could not. "I will certainly do my utmost," she answered.

Matthias slouched negligently in his chair and considered her, his eyes hooded. "Then I will try your herbs, but will promise nothing. Will you send Hornsby to me?" He turned his head, hoping she would leave. She had just refused to marry him and he wanted to lick his wounds. It had not been romantic—was that what she wanted? She had not appeared to consider it or even take it seriously. Marriage to him would make her secure for life, and it would fill his need for a countess. And he…he would know she was safe and provided for.

There was a great deal of unfinished business between them; many words left unspoken. It seemed as though it would be necessary to reopen old wounds. He frowned and shifted his weight, sending what felt like a bolt of lightning through his leg. He sat still, as far as he was able, trying to breathe slow breaths until the gripping pain released a little.

How did Kitty think he could give up the only thing that helped? Besides dulling the pain, it also dulled his mind. When everything else failed, he could not silence his mind—even in sleep.

Having her here again was a double-edged sword. The sweet lavender scent of her took him back to the best days of his life. At times, the three of them were down by the lake, whiling away a long summer's day. But then, just as quickly as a storm rolling in, they were in the midst of war and Kitty was Peter's wife—offering up the constant reminder that she was lost to Matthias forever. And then... then Peter was lost and Kitty a widow...

Loving your best friend's wife was the devil of a situation. The guilt was unbearable.

Back in England, wounded in heart and body, Matthias could have thrown in his hand, until he arrived home to find Kitty installed in his house. Suddenly, he had a chance of her again even though everything was different—and now she had unequivocally rejected him. How could she expect him to give up his only comfort? Something had to be done.

"Yes, my lord?" Hornsby's voice intruded on his self-pity.

"I need to write some letters."

"Would you like me to send for the steward?"

"No, these I must pen myself. Then I would like to be taken outside again. I cannot bear to be within these walls any longer."

"The weather and your mood appear to be kindred spirits this day."

As Hornsby helped him to his desk, Matthias gasped and clenched his jaw in pain. Would this ever get better? It had been two months since he was wounded.

Hornsby did not remark upon it. "Of course, sir. Would you like me to fetch you a book and a blanket?"

"No, just a bottle of brandy."

"That bad, is it, sir?" Hornsby wrongly assumed all the pain was physical. He did not know the three friends' history and it was better that way, although doubtless he would have heard some gossip.

"No pity from you," Matthias commanded brusquely.

"I wouldn't think of it, Major."

"You should be whipped for insolence," Matthias retorted.

"As you have remarked many times, Major."

Matthias did not return the jibe, feeling somehow comforted by the exchange, and Hornsby quietly left him to write his letters. The brethren had always done their best to maintain contact and he wanted to let them know he was alive and Kitty was also at Thackeray Close.

My Dear brethren,

As you know, I was wounded in the final push at La Haye Saint. I remember very little about the past month of my life, but I have survived the fever and am now praying my bone will heal so that I may walk again. I wish to thank each of you for ensuring I returned home in one piece. I am told it took all of your efforts to make that happen.

I was surprised to find Mrs. Gordon here when I arrived. At present, she is well and attempting to convince me she is suited to the role of housekeeper. That is a battle I do not intend to lose.

There is a little else worthy of pen and paper. Do write when it is convenient.

Pietas et honos

Thackeray

"Ah, Hornsby," Matthias said, folding his last letter as his batman entered some little while later. "I should like to attempt to walk with my crutch, with you supporting me on the other side."

"Would it not be wiser to wait for the second crutch?"

"I need to do this, Sergeant." If they were to return to officer and soldier, so be it.

Hornsby grumbled under his breath, but handed him the crutch. Putting Matthias's other arm over his shoulder, Hornsby lifted him upright. They hobbled slowly from the house and after much experimentation eventually found a rough rhythm.

ELIZABETH JOHNS

The walk to the lake was gruelling, but it was what he needed. Facing the reality of his condition was the first step towards returning to a semblance of life.

He settled into the chair by the lake, his body shaking from the exertion and threatening to cast up his breakfast on to the grass.

"Time heals most wounds, Major. It doesn't mean they will be like before."

"Sergeant turned prophet, are we, Hornsby?"

"I have a great many more truisms where that came from," the sergeant retorted. He reached into his pocket and pulled out a bottle of brandy and a bell. "Ring when you are ready... sir."

He walked away, grumbling under his breath.

"Dismissed," Matthias added sardonically to Hornsby's back, but then he was alone with his demons and thoughts. He closed his eyes, but it only served to produce flashing lights that accompanied the throbbing in his leg.

He reached for the bottle; pausing with his hand on the neck, he considered Kitty's words. Did she not understand this was a necessary evil? He removed the lid, then swirled the amber liquid around, watching it coat the sides of the glass. If she could find something to ease the pain he would be grateful, but until then, the liquid fire would have to do.

As long as Kitty was provided for, there was little else he could do bar stay alive so that his brother did not inherit. The thought brought another sharp pain to his chest. He had hoped to have married and had an heir by now. He could not yet face that prospect with a woman other than Kitty. How else might he account for the past when clearly she did not wish to be more than friends?

Having her within reach, seeing her every day in the role of house-keeper and being unable to act upon his feelings would be torture, he mused despondently, but surely it would be better than wondering where she was? It still hurt deeply that she had preferred to go her own way—and live in poverty—than ask him for help.

His father had a great deal to answer for if ever they met again.

Certainly, he had succeeded in making Kitty feel unworthy of being a lady. Matthias muttered a savage oath.

There had been a time when he had believed Kitty returned his affections, but his sire had cast her from the house.

Why had she gone to Peter instead of him? That question would forever haunt him.

～

KITTY SPENT most of her time in the herb garden or still-room, determined to find something to heal Matthias which would not also cause further harm. He seemed appropriately wary of opium's evils, so why was he willing to tempt fate with intoxicating spirits? It was not immediately addictive, it was true, but it could still destroy lives and make a slave of its master.

She had studied Lady Thackeray's book of notes and thought she had at last unearthed some plants to try. Eagerly, she harvested the leaves from the herbs she needed,

She collected comfrey leaves—not the roots or flowers—per Lady Thackeray's warning notes in the margin of the book. Mint was the easiest to use and grew in overabundance. She clipped several bunches, stopping to smell the fresh leaves. The lavender she took care to harvest stems with full blooms, which made a more potent oil, then clipped some rosemary to replenish the supply she would use. Her basket was full of fragrance from minty to pine to floral notes.

She had watched Lady Thackeray prepare herbs many times, but the process seemed arduous and she did not have the time to experiment. Line by line, she followed her ladyship's detailed instructions and was able to produce some credible oils.

After much deliberation, she had decided to use Mr. Satterlee's Indian herb in a cordial for Matthias to drink, a comfrey poultice for the bullet wound, and some oils of lavender, mint and rosemary for Hornsby to massage deep into the tissues to help with pain.

It was a poor testament to the state of medicine if she was attempting to be a healer, but on the battlefield she had seen many times with her own eyes that the sawbones had little skill beyond amputating limbs. It was then left to the patient and fate whether they lived or died from the inevitable fever.

As she went to present her remedies to Matthias, she prayed he was in a receptive mood. If this did not work, then she did not know what to do. She could hardly deny him spirits if she had no better alternative. One thing was for certain, she had never had to endure the physical pain he was suffering, but the emotional pain in addition —she did not know how soldiers could bear it. Losing Peter had been the hardest thing she could have imagined. Everything in her life had been turned upside down in an instant, in addition to losing her husband and friend. But to watch him die then be wounded yourself, whatever must that be like? She knew Matthias needed her help. Had she been faced with the same situation, in all likelihood, she would have turned to drink herself.

She knocked on the door, knowing Hornsby would be present and waiting on his lordship for his morning ablutions.

"Enter," Matthias called.

Kitty turned the latch hoping he was decently garbed, for his own sake. She had certainly seen a gentleman unclothed before.

"Good morning, my lord, Hornsby. I have brought some medicaments I hope will help."

Matthias said nothing, but she recognized the doubt in his face. Ignoring it and persisting, she continued, "I consulted the apothecary and he suggested a special herb from India that is said to help in healing bone. It has been some time since your injury, but perhaps this will help its continued healing. It may taste bitter, but I have made it into one of your mother's cordials which I hope will make it palatable." She set it on the table and continued, scarcely taking a breath. She was nervous and hoped very much it did not show.

Next, she held up a cloth filled with herbs. "This is a poultice of setbone, which is said to, well, help the bone set." She laughed nervously.

Surprisingly, the only protest came when Kitty produced the oils to be massaged into Matthias's leg. She held up a glass vial of golden liquid. "And finally, this is a mixture of herbs to be kneaded into the tissues."

"You never said bein' a valet would mean rubbin' fancy oils all over you like some Sultan's harem." Hornsby conveniently dropped his aitches and pretended offence when convenient.

"Cut line, Hornsby. I will do it myself."

"It matters not who does it, just see that it is done. This mixture of lavender, mint, rosemary, and willow bark is said to help with pain and slow the inflammation that impairs healing."

"How quickly do these things work?" Matthias asked, suddenly interested.

"No doubt slower than you would wish, but the apothecary believed in the herb's properties and your mother's notes on the poultice and oils were very encouraging." It was understandable to doubt medicine, having been a soldier. The only tried and true remedies were laudanum and spirits, and everything else seemed quackery.

Nonetheless, he gave a nod and she turned to leave, satisfied for now that at least her efforts had not been dismissed.

"Mrs. Gordon, you have a caller," Hayes informed her as Kitty reached the bottom of the stairs.

"Who is it?"

"She would not say, ma'am, but she did reveal that you were old acquaintances. I believe her to be Lady Gordon."

Unfortunately, a housekeeper could not simply refuse to see people as a lady could. Kitty stopped and checked her appearance in the mirror in the entrance hall before proceeding, wiping a smudge of dirt from her cheek as she did so. She chuckled. That would never do. No one else had seen it, or at least had not had the gumption to mention it.

She smoothed down her skirts and opened the door to the drawing room. Why she would have a caller in the drawing room instead of the housekeeper's rooms, she did not have time to dwell upon. The woman sitting there, rigid-spined had aged almost beyond recognition. Her once dark hair had greyed and he face was etched deeply with wrinkles that made her resting expression a perpetual scowl.

"Fanny? What are you doing here?" she asked as she closed the door behind her. Sir Nigel's wife was the last person she would have expected to call. While Sir Nigel had always objected to the marriage and treated Kitty with disdain, Fanny had been civil. She had not been a friend to Kitty, or shown warmth like a sister—although there was nothing unusual in that—yet neither had she been an enemy. It seemed that was about to change.

She sniffed, her nose in the air, as though it was beneath her to be here as well. "You may have heard that my husband paid a visit to Lord Thackeray which was less than successful. I thought that I, as a fellow lady..." She hesitated, clearly over including Kitty in that last word. "Might appeal to your better nature."

"My better nature?" Kitty already sensed where this conversation was heading.

"Lord Thackeray is a gentleman and they all have some misguided sense of honour. Although keeping you under his roof unwed is hardly honourable, we do understand why he cannot marry you."

Kitty's bristles were already on end.

"If you choose to be careless with your name and reputation, that is entirely your own affair, but why must you be so with ours?"

That was enough. "Why did you not consider this when I sought you out after Peter's death?"

"We gave you twenty pounds to see you established! If you squandered such a sum, it is not our villainy to be blamed for your situation as you would have me believe!"

Kitty detested arguments; and was there really any point in trying to reason with someone like this? There seemed to be a subdivision of the aristocracy that was born without that ability.

"Lady Gordon, I will assure you the money was not squandered—unless you consider my survival trivial. I did my best to economize, but it is far from easy for a gently bred woman to live on her own without fortune or references. I did the best I could. Of a certainty, I did not squander the funds!"

"Well!" Fanny huffed, clearly affronted.

"Was there anything else?" Kitty no longer had the patience to be civil to someone who could treat her thus.

"I came because I thought you might need a little sisterly advice, but it is clear you will not be reasoned with." Motherly was more like it, Kitty fumed inwardly. Fanny was ten years her senior, but she had never been one to accept her age with grace. "I know you have not had Lady Thackeray's guidance and may not understand the importance of what is being said about you."

"I was married for three years and have been widowed for two. I am well aware of what is said of me—by people who were born with silver spoons in their mouths."

Lady Gordon stood up, a red blotch high on each cheek, the feathers on her bonnet reflecting her annoyance in their movement. "I cannot help you if you will not help yourself. You are, quite brazenly, living in sin, and out of Christian charity I came here to help you save your reputation. I am certain Mr. Henderson will be paying you a visit soon. I wanted first to prevail upon our previous relationship and beg you to reconsider."

"Christian charity? You dare to speak to me in such terms when I was left begging for work like a pauper? I do not think I care to heed such reprimands from those who have more regard for their name and appearance than my welfare. Good day, Lady Gordon." Kitty turned and left the room, hurtling through the house and out towards her garden. Perhaps coming here had been a mistake, but she had set her course and was determined at least to see Matthias healed as well as he could be.

CHAPTER 9

"This is the vilest thing I have ever tasted!" Matthias exclaimed as he attempted to swallow the bitter brew Kitty had prepared for him.

"Do I need to plug your nose and force it down?" Hornsby asked with mock severity.

Matthias tipped his head back and drank the remainder of the dose while glaring at his old batman, who wore a satisfied look on his face.

"Now for the oil," Hornsby announced, looking at the bottle with open scepticism and distaste.

He folded back the sheet to reveal the offending limb. On the surface, it did not look anything like how it felt underneath. Beneath, it felt like a volcano, gurgling hot lava that it was about to cast from its molten depths.

"You mean to touch me with that?"

"Ay, my lord. Much though I do not wish to, I cannot think you will be able to make a proper shift of it."

"It smells...not horrid." He could not quite place the mixture of herbal scents.

"Very medicinal, like," Hornsby added.

"I am afraid to know. Get it over with, then."

Hornsby poured some oil on to his hands, then rubbed them together. He held his hands up and sniffed. "It tingles," he remarked in wonder before rubbing the potion over Matthias's leg.

"It does," he agreed, through clenched teeth. "It also hurts when you clamp down on my leg like an adder trying to kill its prey!"

"Oh, beg pardon, my lord, but she did say to rub it deep into the muscles."

"To relieve pain, not cause it."

Hornsby shrugged, but did ease the pressure of his ministrations.

It was still not comfortable, but Matthias allowed Hornsby to do as Kitty had instructed for a few minutes. Hornsby then placed a poultice of cool, wet herbs over the healing wound and allowed him to rest.

Matthias had just closed his eyes, tired enough to slip back into oblivion, when Hornsby made a noise.

"What is it?"

"Some lady leaving the house in high dudgeon."

"How do you know she is in a huff?" Matthias asked. It was an odd way to describe someone.

"Her back is as straight as a board, her nose is up in the air, and her feet are stamping with every step making them stupid feathers in her bonnet bop up and down like a chicken pecking at its feed."

Matthias frowned. What lady would be calling, alone, on him? It must be to do with Kitty. "Will you go and see what it was about?"

"I thought that was what butlers were for," Hornsby muttered under his breath, but having put away the towels and shaving supplies, departed on the errand.

There were few ladies in the county who Matthias could imagine calling at the Close, especially if they knew he was wounded. He wondered if perhaps the visitor had just left her calling card with good wishes, but no, he recalled that Hornsby had said she looked upset. Matthias groaned. It was very likely Fanny Gordon, come to harass Kitty.

Why could people not mind their own business? He wanted to

wallow in his misery in private, for Kitty's presence had already destroyed any peace of mind he'd had remaining.

But he had not known it would be thus.

Much though he wanted to sulk in his room, he knew that would never do. He also knew that this state of affairs could not endure. If only she would give him some sign of encouragement, he would press his suit. Did it not matter to her that she was under his roof and compromised? She clearly thought she was an independent widow and could recover her reputation with the passage of time.

Would it help smooth ruffled feathers if everyone knew he had proposed and she had refused? No, for she would be branded a jade and having his rejection the subject of idle gossip would certainly not help his pride.

His brethren were all finding wives and settling down—the ones who still lived. He swallowed hard. At this point he was still not certain which was preferable. For some reason, God had chosen for him to live and who was he to nay-say the Lord above?

"I would like to beg a bit of assistance in the way of pain and healing, if you will," he muttered, in case anyone in the heavenly realm was listening.

He took his crutch and hobbled pitifully over to the window. He felt no relief from Kitty's efforts, but it was early yet. It was too much to hope for that anything would bring the instant relief afforded by brandy. He pulled the flask from his pocket and took a deep drink, relishing the immediate alleviation of his hurts.

He took another and then another, and slid down to the floor with his broken leg out in front of him. He had not drunk so much that he failed to be protective of that. Who knew how long it would be until someone came to administer to his needs? He suspected it would be an hour or two at the least. Hornsby had left his correspondence on the bed, but could he read it from here? Matthias flapped at the edge of the counterpane. A couple of letters fluttered to the ground but only one fell within reach unless he shuffled on his rear or began to crawl. He was not yet ready to stoop to that indignity.

Settling for the one he could barely reach with his fingers, bit by bit, finger by finger, he slid it close enough that he could reach it.

He opened it and though the words were somewhat blurred, he immediately knew Henry was causing trouble again. He had become all too familiar with the Dean of his younger brother's Oxford College.

Henry was being expelled. Again.

How much would it take to convince them to keep him this time? Would, perhaps, an appeal from a wounded soldier, accompanied by a generous donation, put them off for a bit longer? He could not bear to deal with Kitty, his wounds and his rapscallion excuse for an heir all at the same time.

Dunford would have to deal with the letter whenever he arrived to go through the estate books. It seemed, however, that by that juncture Henry could have built and paid for his own separate college at the place of the hallowed white stones.

There was little else Matthias could do without pen and paper, or two good legs to distract him from the ever-present pain. He drained the dregs of the flask and leaned back against the wall in light-headed bliss, having not a care now for his woes. Smiling foolishly, he allowed his mind to go back to those days when they had all been happy; when he thought Kitty felt the same as he.

He had thought back so many times, to seek what he might have done differently…

On this occasion his thoughts took him to the night of the midsummer ball. The night had felt magical: warm and fragrant, the time of year when the sky was never darker than dusk due to the stars twinkling down on them. They had danced and laughed, and made promises that neither of them could keep. After the ball they had sneaked out to the lake and had lain on a blanket under the sky, talking and kissing for hours. On their return, the Earl had been waiting for them, and had accused Kitty of countless horrible things—to include seducing and trying to entrap Matthias so she could be a countess. Even though he had assumed the worst, he had no thought to preserving Kitty's honour. The look on Kitty's face that night still haunted Matthias. Her disappointment in him was worse than any other punishment could have been. The more Matthias protested, the angrier his father had become. He'd sent Matthias to his chambers, and Kitty had been banished from the house.

Besides his father, Matthias had only himself to blame. Naïvely, he had thought his father would accept Kitty into the family since she had been brought up under his own roof. Instead, the old Earl had behaved as if such an idea was preposterous and bordering on incestuous. He had threatened to disown Matthias if he defied him.

Matthias had been studying law at the time and knew he could not be disinherited, but had not wanted to sever the connexion with his father, his only remaining parent.

The incident had ruined their relationship anyway.

It had all happened so fast. Matthias had still been convinced he could change the Earl's mind when he had heard the shocking news. But Kitty had not waited for him to make things right. Matthias's heart had been broken, but Peter had come to the rescue. He had purchased a commission and was leaving for the Peninsula; he had at once offered to take Kitty with him.

In a fit of anger, Matthias had bought his own commission and followed them. He had not known what he expected to find, but by the time he had reached them, they were already married. What could he have done but congratulate them? It was not as though he could have called his best friend out for being a gentleman. Instead, he had acted as though nothing had happened.

Peter had never said a word to him about the matter, though he must have known.

Yet the doubts lingered still. Had Kitty ever loved Peter as more than a friend? She proclaimed to love them both, but what did that mean? Did she have any feelings left for himself—beyond those of a brotherly kind—after all these years and all that had happened? These were the thoughts which always tormented him when he sat alone in silence.

"Matthias?" He heard her voice, but was it real or just a dream?

He did not wish to open his eyes, but he felt a hand shaking him and, reluctantly, forced himself to look.

Her amber eyes searched his. She was so close he could feel her breath. "Kitty," he whispered, "I—"

"You are drunk!" she growled angrily.

He shrugged, the movement making his head spin. "Your herbs didn't work," he explained, the alcohol loosening his tongue. Normally, he would have attempted to use a modicum of tact.

Her eyes filled with disappointment—a look he recognized, having seen it just now in his mind's eye. It felt like a knife to his chest. Instead of lashing out at him in anger, she helped him to his feet and settled him on the bed, a closeness he would have appreciated more had he not just hurt her.

Tight-lipped, she helped him lift his broken leg up on to the bed. Then, thrusting a decanter of brandy from a nearby tray into his hand, she exited the room without a backwards glance.

~

KITTY SOUGHT solace in the garden. It was the only place she felt she belonged. The servants were still uncomfortable in her presence, yet neither was she the lady of the house. Why had she thought she could be friends with Matthias again, that five years of hurt could be erased?

Matthias was very different from Peter. Peter had been much simpler in his thoughts and emotions. That had been a small blessing, not having to guess what he was thinking. He was a soldier and hunting enthusiast, and as long as he could do one or the other he was happy. He had treated Kitty as well as he was able. Mostly, she reflected, he had not thought much about her at all. For herself, being married to a friend out of pity had been awkward and she had done everything she could to show her appreciation by learning to cook and having a clean place for him to come home to at night. They had managed to rub along well enough, although there had never been any romance. It had comfortable enough, and she still mourned him.

Matthias, on the other hand, was a much quieter, more deliberate person who thought deeply about things. He took his responsibilities seriously, and felt the weight of his duties on his shoulders.

Things had never been the same between any of them once she'd had to marry Peter, and that had hurt the most. The loss of her best friend, and what she had thought was her love, had been hard to bear. She had not recovered yet. Loving someone did not mean it was reciprocated, but she still wanted to try her best for him.

Truly, she had no right to tell Matthias what to do, or to be angry that he had found refuge from his pain in a bottle. It simply meant her remedies were not working; at least, not immediately. She knew most remedies took weeks at best, and she'd expected him to stop the one thing that worked for him.

It was hard not to feel defeated, but the work had just begun.

With a heavy sigh, she tended the garden, absently cutting off dead flowers and pulling up weeds, refusing to believe some of the remedies she had given Matthias would not work. But would he continue to use them?

"Miss Kitty?" called Thomas, the footman, disturbing the dangerous pathway of her thoughts.

"I am here," she said, rising from where she had knelt to attend the lavender.

"Mr. Bailey has delivered another crutch, ma'am. He begs your pardon but he was not able to stay to deliver it into your hands." The young man held out the polished wooden stick.

"That is quite understandable. Thank you, Thomas." She accepted the crutch and held it to her chest. She should take it to Matthias, but she did not know if she wanted to see him again so soon, not when they had parted on such bad terms.

Reluctantly, she knew could no more hold back something which would enable him to be mobile than she could withhold fresh milk from a new-born babe.

As she entered the house, part of her hoped she would find Hornsby along the way to do the errand for her, but fortune did not favour her. He was nowhere to be seen, doubtless attending to his duties, and she had no good reason—other than pride—to take him away from them.

She knocked on the door, partly hoping Matthias was sleeping off his potations.

"Enter," a gruff voice replied.

He looked up and appeared surprised to see her again.

She stepped into the room, leaving the door wide open. "Mr. Bailey has delivered your other crutch." She held it out as if it were a peace offering.

"Another torture device," he remarked in a short tone.

"Or a means by which to walk again," she retorted.

"If the bone ever heals." He snarled the words.

She tossed it on the bed at him. "I thought you were the one who requested it? If you prefer to stay bedridden for the rest of your days, it is nothing to me!" Falser words were never spoken, but her tongue sometimes ran ahead of her and she had lashed out in anger.

"I may not have a choice," he snapped.

"You certainly will not if you are in your cups all the time!"

"Recall that the doctor said I should rest! And if your remedies worked, I should not need to drink!"

She put her hands on her hips "It is not the same thing, and you know it. Besides, you need not be *floored* to have some relief from the pain!"

He snorted. "None of us ever put any faith in the sawbones, so why do you believe your potions will work?" he asked, his manner accusatory and condescending. Who was this man who lay hurling insults at her?

"Irrespective of the fact that herbs have been used for centuries, because I trust Mr. Satterlee and your mother more than any army doctor! If you could see your mother's notes, you would understand she had a great deal of knowledge, and I have heard tell of some of the Indian remedies being quite powerful."

"From the British apothecary," he noted dryly.

"If you must know, yes! Mr. Satterlee has studied them at great length. It was through good medicine that your leg has been saved thus far, and it cannot hurt to try." She threw up her hands and walked to the window.

"It most certainly can! I wonder how many people die every year because of quacks? I am sure Waterloo has nothing on them!" he barked bitterly.

Why was he being so stubborn? "I know accepting this injury is difficult, but it is early days yet." It was hard for her to watch Matthias trying to accept his new condition. He looked defeated, a mere shadow of his former self. He had been so full of life and vitality. Was that gone forever?

"I am well aware of every passing moment. I am also not naïve enough to believe I will walk and ride again as before. I may never do either, and both of us will have to accept that! If you are only here to pity me, then you can save your breath!"

"I am trying to help you, *my lord*. If it is unwelcome, then I will see to my duties and leave you to your brandy." Kitty turned and walked briskly from the bedchamber, closing the door behind her.

"Kitty!" She heard him call after her, a note of alarm in his voice, but she could not face him any longer just now. She also needed to accept that neither of them were the same people they were before, and some of their injuries were not visible.

CHAPTER 10

*M*atthias's head was pounding like the devil. Why had he drunk so much? Partly for pain, partly to forget, if truth be known. But it had not worked. He could still remember. He had been an absolute wretch to Kitty.

He did not think they had ever argued like that before. Neither could he account for his beastly behaviour, other than he was trying to accept that he might never walk again... never mind the fact that he had to see her every day and not have her. It was still no excuse and while he knew the drink was partially to blame, he was nevertheless a gentleman and she deserved better.

Somehow he would have to learn to deal with her presence; he could not hide in his chamber for the rest of his days. Indeed, he must needs learn how to get about again. It was too much to bear, to think he would be like this forever.

He reached for the crutches, knowing he should make an attempt. Soldiers with worse injuries than his were able to use them, if they could get them.

Having fingered the smooth wood for a moment or two, he made a decision and rang for Hornsby, who arrived a few minutes later with an ewer of warm water.

"Good morning, Major," the batman said, eyeing his condition thoughtfully.

"Why are you looking at me like that?"

"You have that look in your eye I haven't seen in some time. I was not sure what I would find, having 'eard you and Mrs. Gordon arguing when I came to wait on you last evening. Then, when you did not ring for me..." His voice trailed away.

Never one to mince his words, was Hornsby. Matthias did not answer the batman's accusatory tone.

"My second crutch has arrived. I would like to go to the hunting lodge for a few days and I wish my destination to be kept quiet. Ask Cook to send enough food for a sennight."

The batman looked sideways at him. "What has the hunting lodge to do with your crutches?"

"Does it matter?"

Hornsby scratched his head, and offering no reply, began shaving Matthias. Nonetheless, he grumbled the whole time about toffs and their being dicked in the nob. Once Matthias was dressed, Hornsby helped him downstairs for breakfast. Thankfully, there was no sign of Kitty. Matthias knew he should apologize to her before he left, but suspected she was avoiding him this morning.

"The carriage is awaiting your pleasure, sir," Hornsby announced in a slightly mocking tone some half-an-hour later.

"I gather you do not wish to accompany me? Feel free to stay behind."

Hornsby looked offended. "Of course I will go where you go, Major."

Tossing his napkin on the table, Matthias took the crutches and carefully placed them under his arms. He attempted one step slowly, and as he took the next, the crutches completely slipped out from underneath him, causing him to lose his balance and slam into the ground.

The pain took the breath from him. It hurt too much even to curse.

Hornsby was immediately behind him, trying to help him to his feet.

"Give me a moment," Matthias said through gritted teeth, waving him off.

Hornsby backed away, understanding Matthias's need to have a moment to collect himself. He picked up the crutches and looked them over, placing them on his own arms to see how they worked.

"I suppose these take a bit of practice," he remarked absently as he tried them for himself.

Matthias tried not to be annoyed when his man quickly found a rhythm and was soon going back and forth—in a remarkably smooth fashion—across the breakfast room carpet on the crutches. He glared until Hornsby finally stopped and gave him a sheepish look.

"I have the advantage of learning with two good legs, Major."

"Quite," Matthias said curtly. "I am ready to depart." The sooner, the better, he reflected, casting a sour glance about him from his undignified position.

Hornsby bent down and lifted Matthias from behind. "I shall lean on you, if you please." He could not bear to be carried at this moment.

As they stumbled from the breakfast room to the entrance hall, Matthias noticed the servants were avoiding looking at him. Were they afraid of him—or worse, ashamed of him?

He heard footsteps approaching quickly from behind his batman but did not turn to look.

"You are leaving, my lord?" Kitty asked, her gaze flickering to the waiting conveyance as she came to stand beside them.

He needed to apologize, but this was not the time nor the place. He also needed privacy for a few days, yet he did not want her to think he was running away from her.

"Yes, we will be gone about a week. Dunford can send a message if you have urgent need of me."

"Yes, my lord," she said, curtsying deeply. He did not meet her gaze, because he did not want to see the hurt he knew would be in her eyes.

Hornsby helped him into the carriage and before they had proceeded far down the drive, Matthias was regretting his decision. He was green with pain, his sickly countenance staring back at him from the silver cap on his brandy flask. It was several miles to the hunting lodge, but he needed to remove himself from the house. He needed to learn to use the crutches; he needed to learn to handle the pain—and he needed to find a way to accept Kitty back into his life. They could not go on as they were.

When Hornsby opened the door upon their arrival, Matthias had never been so grateful to see the red brick house with its simple white portico. It was modest in comparison to the Close, with only eight guest rooms.

"You do not look well, Major."

"I do not feel well, Sergeant. It makes me wish I were unconscious again."

Hornsby shook his head. "I hope this place has the magical healing powers you seem to think it does. I gather that's the reason for our being here?"

"This place has a decided lack of people in it."

"Ah, we are running away from Mrs. Gordon, then."

Matthias opened his mouth to argue, but then stopped himself. "Yes," he admitted. "It is difficult to have her in the house."

"Because she cares too much?" Hornsby asked. "A lot of people care, you should know."

"It is more than that."

Hornsby rubbed his chin. "Wondered if that might be the case. Well, you can't hide forever, but we are here for now."

Matthias did not bother scolding Hornsby for his impertinence. It would do little good, and he was correct anyway, curse him. They hobbled up the three steps and he unlocked the door to the empty house. His decision to leave had been sudden, with no time to send staff ahead to prepare. It was just what he needed.

Matthias rested in the first chair they came to, still in Holland covers, while Hornsby brought in their belongings. All the previous night Matthias had lain awake, thinking about Kitty's words.

His behaviour had been that of a stranger. Never before had he been so surly, and she had only said the things she had because she cared. Now he realized he had to do something, because he did not want to stay this way. It was nigh impossible for him to curb his churlishness while she was his housekeeper. She had overturned every gentlemanly principle he had ever been taught... and how could he possibly separate the hurt of her rejection from his physical hurt when her presence endangered his very soul? He needed a few days to think.

When Hornsby returned to see how he did, Matthias had resolved to learn to manage on the crutches at the very least. Hopefully, by managing the physical, he would better handle the rest.

"Hornsby, I wish to go into the open meadow behind the house. There used to be a paddock adjoining it which should be as good a place as any to practicce."

Hornsby grinned, revealing a wide gap between his front teeth. "Aye, Major. But first, you have to take your medicine like a good boy." He held the up the vile cordial Kitty had made.

"Cordial is the greatest misnomer to date." Matthias scowled but swallowed the medicine, chasing it down with some brandy.

They spent two hours out in the field until Matthias learned to manage a few steps with the crutches without putting weight on his broken leg, or having the crutches slip out from under him.

"By Jove, I think you finally have it!" Hornsby praised.

"*Finally...*" Matthias exaggerated the word. "...and I am covered in bruises and blisters for my pains."

"Mayhap in a few days you won't notice them."

Matthias hoped that in a few months he would not need them, but kept the sentiment to himself. At least he still had his leg. "There is a stream over that rise we can bathe in." Matthias pointed. "It should be refreshing at this time of the year. "

"And it'll save me from haulin' in a bath for you," Hornsby said with a grin.

"That, too, Sergeant."

Once they were in the water, Matthias sat back and allowed it to flow across his body, relishing the coolness after his heated exertions.

"It almost feels as though we're back on the Peninsula, don't it?" Hornsby was carving a stick as he sat in the stream.

"Do you miss it?"

He shrugged. "Things seemed simpler. I didn't mind it."

"Do you wish to go back?" Matthias had not thought to ask; he had been so consumed with his own misery. "I appreciate your devotion in seeing me home, but you have no obligation to stay."

"I know. I think it's just hard changing positions, like."

"Yes. I know what you mean."

"'Sides, I do like the food and comfortable bed at the Close."

With that, he sprang from his spot under the water and speared a fish, laughing with glee and as naked as the day he was born. Unfortunately, he was no longer a babe.

"Hornsby! For the love of all that is holy, put some clothes on!" Matthias covered his face as though to hide the sight.

His old batman just laughed. He held up a good-sized trout. "I caught us some dinner!"

∾

KITTY TRIED to pretend nothing was out of the ordinary when Matthias left, but she was concerned that the servants would not listen to her whilst he was gone. She need not have worried on that score; the house still operated in a seamless fashion and the other servants treated her with deference. Despite this, she felt more isolated than before Matthias had left. "But at least you have a warm bed and plenty of food to eat," she reminded herself. Added to that, she had independence and the freedom to roam the estate... and be alone with her thoughts.

One benefit of working your fingers to the bone was you were too tired to dwell on your grief and misery. Everyone in the workhouses and shops had seemed to have problems worse than hers, so she had numbed herself to all feeling and survived as best she could. It was better not to think about how she had been cast from her childhood home, how her husband and best friend had died, and now, how the only person she had left did not want her in the house.

Still, she was determined to see him improved, and to that end set out that morning to visit Mr. Satterlee again.

"Good morning, Miss Kitty. What may I do for you?" he greeted her.

"The herbs are not working fast enough, I am afraid," she said as she approached the counter.

He wore an sympathetic look on his face as he pulled his glasses off. "Even if they work, it will take time—weeks, months even. There is never a guarantee, and we do not know precisely what is wrong. Perhaps the bone is not broken and there is some other damage to the tissues which is causing his lordship's problems."

Kitty's heart sank. "So it is best to continue with what we are doing? I prepared the herb as you prescribed, in addition to the poultice. I also found one of lady Thackeray's receipts for an oil preparation to be rubbed into the tissues."

"It certainly cannot do any harm. I imagine the immobility, and the forming of adhesions in the tissues, would benefit from the emulsion's properties and movement."

Kitty exhaled a deep breath.

"You are doing all you can, my dear," he said in a kind, fatherly way.

"I am afraid I made a mistake in coming back here." She swallowed hard and wondered why she was opening her heart to this man, but he was one of the few who was still showing her kindness. "Nevertheless, I cannot leave until I know I have tried."

"Lady Thackeray would be very proud of you."

Kitty was not so certain, but what else could she say? "Thank you. Good day, Mr. Satterlee."

She stepped back outside, remembering that the last time she left the shop she had chanced upon Sir Nigel. Although she had expected further interference from them, nothing had been forthcoming. Had Fanny not said the rector would call? Perhaps her own earlier visit to Mrs. Henderson had helped, at least to some degree, but would Kitty be welcomed at church? Even servants were allowed to go to services.

Unfortunately, she was not certain she was brave enough to make the attempt on her own, but avoiding church would only give the tabbies more reason to talk. There were a few people out on the street, going about their business. Was it too much to hope no one would recognize her?

Kitty stopped in the middle of the street. "This is ridiculous," she said aloud, not caring who heard her. She made an about face and walked to the end of the street, towards the church and rectory.

She held her hand up to knock, then stepped back and waited. As before, Mrs. Jones answered the door and dropped into a curtsy fit for a lady.

"Are Mr. or Mrs. Henderson at home?" Kitty inquired.

"Who's there, Jones?" Mrs. Henderson called from the sitting room to the side of the front entrance. "Is that Miss Kitty?"

"Yes, ma'am," the maid returned and held open the door with a smile and a guiding hand.

At least the door had not been closed in her face, Kitty thought in relief. Slightly encouraged, she walked into the room. "Good day, Mrs. Henderson," she said, walking over to take the lady's hands, knowing she could not see her.

"Jones, please bring some tea. Do you be seated," she said to Kitty with old-fashioned formality.

"Thank you. Forgive my calling unannounced, Mrs. Henderson. I was in the village and thought I would look in on you."

"I am glad you did. How is his lordship?"

"He is well enough but his leg is not healing fast enough to suit him." Kitty hoped no one offered to call in the next few days. She could hardly tell them he had run away from her, could she?

"He always was an active lad. He and Mr. Peter were both spirited boys," she said fondly. "And you, such a scrawny mite when you arrived."

"I did my best to keep up." Kitty chuckled. Oh, to have those carefree days back again. It was another lifetime entirely.

"We pray daily that his leg will heal."

The maid brought in the tea and set it on the table between them. "Would you pour, my dear?"

"Of course, ma'am." Kitty poured the tea and remembered the milk and spoonful of sugar that Mrs. Henderson took. She placed the cup in the lady's hands, then made her own and resumed her seat. She took the first sip, which was always her favourite, then steeled herself to speak of the dreadful topic on everybody's lips. "Mrs. Henderson, you must know what is being said about me in the village. It is worse than I expected. My brother-in-law has turned against me and is convinced I am living in sin at Thackeray Close."

"He said this to you?"

"He said it to his lordship, but Lady Gordon accused me directly. I do not wish to cause trouble for anyone, and I would like to attend services. However, I fear my presence may result in unpleasantness. I did not expect my position at the Close to cause such a rift. I am a widow, after all, and I am living there honourably."

Mrs. Henderson looked confused.

"Did Sir Nigel not come to speak with the Rector?"

"I am not privy to all of my husband's conversations, but he did not speak ill of you in church. Quite the contrary, in fact."

"I beg your pardon?"

"Allow me to request the Rector to join us, in case I am misinformed. Sir Nigel did call here a few days ago, but he was not ill-tempered at all."

Kitty frowned. Mrs. Henderson rang the small bell on the table beside her chair, then directed the maid to find the rector. They sipped their tea in silence while Kitty tried to unravel this mystery. Sir Nigel had definitely left the Close in an angry and threatening humour.

Footsteps were heard approaching across the parquet floor, and Kitty's pulse began to throb with nervousness. The cup began to tremble in her hand, so she placed it back on the table.

The Rector entered the room and smiled at her. "Mrs. Gordon, what a pleasant surprise." Kitty stood up and grasped his hands, which were held out to her in a most informal manner. His hair was now grey and he stooped, but it was good to see the gentleman she had spent so much time with as a child, whilst taking her lessons alongside the boys.

The greeting certainly did not indicate condemnation.

97

"Would you care for a cup of tea, sir?" Kitty asked, already knowing the answer and knowing precisely how much milk and sugar he liked as well. He gave her a nod and then sat down on an arm chair.

"Silas, could you please explain to Miss Kitty what Sir Nigel said to you when he paid his recent visit?"

Kitty handed him his cup and her hand began to shake again.

"Why, he came to tell me that you and Lord Thackeray are to be married."

Kitty choked on the tea she was sipping.

"Are you quite well, my dear?" Mrs. Henderson asked.

"Yes, yes. The tea had gone the wrong way." She coughed a few more times. How dare Sir Nigel do such a thing? Was he trying to force her hand? Matthias could call him out for such a thing. Of course, Matthias had offered, but Kitty did not believe his proposal had been sincere. She was not interested in another marriage of convenience. "And Sir Nigel has made the entire village privy to this news, I presume?"

"Oh, yes," Mrs. Henderson said. "He told everyone after the services on Sunday. He said he could not be more pleased for Peter's widow."

No doubt, she thought, most uncharitably. Was it not just like Nigel to try to manipulate Kitty into making this a beneficial arrangement for him? He would prey on that connexion as much as he were able.

"Are you disappointed, my dear? Was it to be kept secret?" Mrs. Henderson asked. No wonder she had been confused by Kitty's earlier statements.

"I do not believe it is something Sir Nigel should be informing people on my behalf." That was an understatement. What was Kitty to do? She needed to speak with Matthias, and soon. This was not just her muddle to clean up.

"Perhaps not, indeed, but do let me be the first to say how pleased we are for you. We had always hoped for this match," Mrs. Henderson said, oblivious to Kitty's turmoil.

So had I, her inner voice wailed. Yet what could she say to these kind people? Kitty stood to leave. "Thank you. I must be going, now. It was lovely to see you again."

"Please let me know when would be a good time to call," Mr. Henderson requested, shaking her hand. "If I may be so bold as to put myself forward as your spiritual guide, the sooner I do so the better. People will talk, you know."

Oh, yes, indeed. There was never any doubt of it—and whatever would they say when they discovered there was no betrothal?

CHAPTER 11

"Have a care, now," Hornsby said as Matthias slipped a little. Over the past several days he had improved his stability with the crutches and, as a result, his mobility.

"Yes, yes," Matthias retorted. "You are worse than my riding master."

"Well, you are one of the finest horsemen I've ever seen, so there must be something to it."

"You always did have to turn things to your good."

"And why not, Major, if it's true?" Hornsby had perfected impudence.

Matthias simply shook his head. He hobbled over to the paddock rail and leaned against it.

"Don't you think you might be good enough to go home yet? We have been here nearly a week," the batman asked.

Matthias did not know if he was·ready to go back. There was something peaceful and simple about being here at the lodge. At home, there were complications. Nevertheless, he knew he could not avoid Kitty forever. "I need to learn how to do stairs," he answered, rather than face reality just yet.

"Then inside we go. You ain't going to learn them out here."

Stairs were impossible. It was precarious enough having to balance one's weight on the crutches, but to do it on such a small platform, with the knowledge it meant certain death if you failed? Matthias lost his courage after attempting the first step about ten times. "I think I had better wait until I can put weight on this leg." He sank down on to the second step and leaned against the banister, his arms and legs shaking from exertion.

"Aye," Hornsby agreed. "But then it means you can no longer avoid going home, or at least admitting why."

"It is complicated," Matthias said. "It is not so simple as accepting I may never walk or ride again. Returning here brings back memories of a different life, one that held hope and possibility and now reminds me of all I have lost."

Hornsby just stared at him.

"I fear I have gone maudlin. 'Tis what you deserve for asking."

"You may be forgiven a little of that," Hornsby said, "but I think you will a walk again and perhaps even ride. Just consider how much you have improved in a few days. I believe Mrs. Gordon's remedies are helping. You have drunk barely one bottle of brandy in the entire week."

Matthias eyed him, looking sideways without turning his head. Perhaps that was true. Even with the extra exercise, he had not needed to drown himself in liquor.

"You will have to deal with her, you know. You cannot ignore her forever."

Matthias snorted. "You think I do not know that? Do you understand what it was like to see her married to Peter? Every day, for three long years, I was jealous of my best friend! And then for two years she preferred to starve than ask for my help. Even now she is only here because she had no other alternative."

"It is clear she cares for you, Major," Hornsby said quietly.

"But only as a brother."

"Does she know how you feel? Mayhap she cherishes warmer thoughts but does not feel she has the right to tell you. Have you considered trying to woo her? If I may be frank—"

Matthias snorted. "When have you ever jibbed at that?"

"I never could abide mealy-mouthed fools," he said simply. "What I have heard pass between you would not make me think you had tender feelings..."

Matthias had had enough and did not wish to delve deeper into the matter. He forced himself up on to his good leg and hobbled away. "Let us be gone, then."

He scrambled out onto the portico in his ungainly manner and waited for Hornsby to pack up their belongings and harness the horses to the carriage.

Walking into a room with a smooth, confident gait would never happen again, he reflected. Instead, he would receive looks of pity. Of all the things he had taken for granted, he had never considered how it might be to be crippled! Much though it grated, Hornsby was right about many things. The batman had never held from speaking his mind, and knowing he could trust Hornsby's advice was better than a purse of gold.

Now he had to become reconciled with his feelings for Kitty or he was doomed to misery. Could Hornsby be right? Had he been nothing but a boor to her? Would she be more receptive to him if he treated her the way he wanted to? He did not know if love was possible. If she had loved Peter as he himself loved her, there might not be room for that kind of romance in her heart... but Matthias needed to marry—needed a proper heir—and he had never been able to consider anyone else for his wife.

It would certainly mean swallowing his pride. He knew she loved him as a brother and at one time he had thought she returned his feelings. Then doubt had replaced the anger he had initially felt at her marriage and he had remembered her also laughing and dancing with Peter. Had she kissed him the same way too—whispered promises with him in the way she had with Matthias? He would not have thought her capable of duplicity, but the pain of seeing her with Peter had been worse than anything he was experiencing now.

He sighed. It was all in the past and it was time he allowed it to stay there. Peter was dead and the two of them had only each other now. The thought of her leaving again was untenable.

What would it take to convince her to have him? The thought of her as his servant was ridiculous. 'Twas more than ridiculous—preposterous, provoking, infuriating—soul-crushing.

Maybe he could do everything in his power and still might not change her mind. He looked down at himself. Clothed and still, he did not appear too different—because no one could see the scars. Somehow, he did not think Kitty would care about that.

But what did she care about? What would it take to change her mind?

"What are you thinking about, Major? You look as if you were back on the Peninsula, plotting the downfall of the Frogs," Hornsby said, having brought the carriage around and pulled the horses to a stop.

"I was plotting a strategy," Matthias confessed with a wry look.

"This sounds promising," Hornsby answered, jumping down to help Matthias.

"Let me try by myself," he said quickly, before Hornsby went to the trouble of tying up the horses.

The batman stood back, understanding Matthias' need to be independent. It was a large part of healing.

"Are you going to tell me what scheme you are brewing in your canister?" Hornsby asked, watching as Matthias managed to climb into the vehicle by himself, no matter how ungracefully.

"I am considering how to convince Miss Kitty that she wants to be my wife," he said, trying to catch his breath as he fell on to the squabs.

Hornsby flashed his gap-toothed grin. "Oh, you have an hour or two to come up with something!"

"If you happen to have any suggestions..." Matthias left the thought dangling. He had never wanted to marry anyone but Kitty. He enjoyed flirtations with some of the ladies who followed the drum, but none of them had so much as tempted him.

"I have never wooed a lady, but it seems to me that most females like to be romanced and what not." Hornsby waved his hand in the air. "Flowers, poems, dancing and the like."

"I shall not be dancing in the near future," Matthias grumbled.

"Maybe not, but you did ask." Hornsby closed the door, leaving Matthias to his thoughts. He found fault with himself every mile of the journey back to the manor house. He tried his hardest to recollect what Kitty had liked as a girl. She had been close to his mother, then after she passed away, Kitty had followed Peter and himself like a lost puppy.

He frowned. He could not actually recall anything in particular Kitty was partial to other than puddings.

Did she like to read? Did she have a favourite flower? "I should know these things." He was doomed to failure. There was no one he could ask. Perhaps Mrs. Harlow would know, but how long would it take for a letter to reach her and then she respond?

As each mile passed, he grew more nervous. His palms were sweaty and he had tugged his neckcloth loose by the time they pulled into the drive.

Part of him was desperate for a glimpse of Kitty, but part of him needed more time to come up with a plan—a battle strategy. Two hours had not been nearly long enough. However, fate decreed she was standing on the steps when the carriage pulled to a stop. Even when he had first seen her, she had still been beautiful, but now, after enough rest and good food, she was once more in full bloom. Despite that horrid grey house-keeper's gown, she was the most beautiful woman in the world to him.

Hornsby held open the door and Matthias gave him a look intended to convey he did not want help. He could succeed. It was necessary for him to learn.

Kitty had been moving forward but when she saw him, stopped and watched.

He wished he had practised climbing out of the carriage. It seemed much harder than climbing in. He still could not manage any weight on his injured leg, but he put his good leg down and then was able to lean forward on his crutches to bear the rest of his weight. He gained the ground in a rather ungainly fashion, but fortunately without falling.

He looked up and cast a shy smile at Kitty, feeling rather proud of himself.

To his chagrin she missed it entirely, for she rushed forward, looking distressed. "The whole village thinks we are betrothed!"

~

KITTY DID NOT KNOW what she had been hoping for, but Matthias's smile faded.

"I rather hoped you would notice my progress!"

"I have been waiting a week to tell you this and that is all you have to say?"

"And I have been working hard to learn to use crutches. I thought you would be pleased."

"Of course, I am. It may not matter to you, but I have been terribly distraught, not knowing what to do and not wanting to make matters worse. Come inside for some coffee and I will admire your prowess with the crutches."

She heard him make a little growl, but she turned around and watched as he managed to walk into the house. It was a vast improvement from the last occasion she had seen him. His colour was better and his speech was quite sober.

Following him into the drawing room, she asked Hayes for the coffee as they passed through the entrance hall. Matthias stood next to a chair and she realized he was waiting for her to sit down first. She quickly perched on a stiff-backed armchair and waved for him to do the same. The relief on his face was palpable, so she knew he must still be in pain.

"That was your reason for leaving, then, to learn how to use your crutches? Where did you go?"

"I felt relations between us were becoming strained and I needed time for reflection, as well as not to make a fool of myself before others. After you brought the second crutch to me, I attempted to use them and promptly fell on my backside."

Kitty was not quite sure what he was trying to tell her. "You have returned, so I presume that means you are satisfied with your progress?" she remarked, finishing on a note of enquiry.

"Enough for now. I still cannot manage the stairs," he said with a sheepish grin which made her heart melt. She had not seen that grin for five years. She caught herself staring at his lean, handsome face and looked away.

Hayes brought in the coffee and a tea tray and Kitty immediately served Matthias. She did not take one for herself.

"You love tea. Why do you not have some?" he asked.

She sighed. He was going to make this impossible. "Have you ever had tea with your housekeeper before?"

"I cannot recall," he said playfully, "but I have taken tea with you before."

She shook her head. "Do be serious. We must do something about this situation."

"I was most deliberately trying not to be serious. I was trying a new approach to my recovery."

"A good attitude is definitely beneficial," Kitty agreed, "but this cannot fadge if you will not accept me as your servant."

"I am trying to, Kitty, but it goes against every part of my being. I do not want you to be my servant, but neither do I want you to leave."

The words warmed Kitty's heart more than they ought. She quickly brought him back to the matter in hand. "It was very wrong of Sir Nigel to say those things."

"He is responsible for the rumours in the village?" Matthias asked with a haughty elevation of one eyebrow.

"Yes. It seems he was telling everyone at church. I found out from Mrs. Henderson when I was in the village last week."

Matthias leaned forward and picked up the pot of tea and poured Kitty a cup. He poured in milk but no sugar. He remembered. A tiny thrill made her breath catch. As he handed it to her, his expression said, 'Don't you dare refuse.'

Giving him a look of exasperation in return, she accepted it but almost dropped the cup when their hands touched. She met his gaze, which was watching her intently. He had felt it too... but what did it mean?

Feelings assailed her like the ones she'd had that summer when she had felt young and invincible; feelings which were not real and could only lead to heartache. She drew back and sat rigidly in the chair.

"Kitty..."

"I beg your pardon, my lord, I almost forgot. There is a messenger here, come urgently to see you. He says he has come from Oxford."

"Henry," Matthias groaned. "What has he done now?"

"Now? Has Henry been in trouble? I know he was full of mischief when he was younger, but surely he has grown out of that?" Kitty asked.

"Hardly. If only Father had not indulged him so much. The boy has not an ounce of conscience for aught unless it is for his own pleasure."

Kitty frowned. She had spent quite a lot of time with Henry when he was small, after Peter and Matthias had gone off to school. "Hopefully it is only a silly prank such as young men are wont to indulge in," she suggested reasonably.

"I never did," he retorted.

"No, but you were brought up to know your duty and what you would inherit, unlike a second son, whose main purpose is to be available. It does not excuse poor behaviour, of course, but perhaps explains why he has been prone to getting into scrapes."

Matthias shook his head, as though it explained nothing. She was sure it must be difficult to comprehend for someone who had always had their future set out for them.

Hayes showed the messenger into the room. He was dressed in buckskin breeches and top-boots, which were liberally covered in dust.

"My lord, my lady." The man bowed deeply.

Kitty realized the man had mistaken her for the countess since she was taking tea with the Earl. Heat flooded her cheeks and she looked at her lap, willing it to fade.

"What has my brother done now?" Matthias did not hide the exasperation from his tone.

The man moved forward and handed him a letter. Matthias read silently before looking up to explain.

"He fought a duel and has fled to the Continent!"

Kitty watched Matthias's face. He had suffered so much and now his brother and heir was once more up to no good. Even Kitty would not have thought Henry capable of such a trick.

"Is the opponent dead?"

"He was not expected to live when I departed for here."

"Thank you for making such haste to inform me. I will send someone to collect my brother's belongings."

"That will not be necessary, my lord. I have brought them with me."

Kitty gasped at the presumption, but Matthias seemed unsurprised.

"If you would like refreshments and to rest before your return journey, Hayes will see you accommodated."

The messenger, whom Kitty assumed to be a confidant of the Dean of Henry's college, bowed and went away with Hayes.

Kitty said nothing, because Matthias was one to think over a matter. He would try to consider things carefully from every angle.

After a few moments of looking out of the window in contemplation, he turned back to her. "I should be more shocked, but I am only surprised it has not happened sooner."

"Will he ever be able to return?"

"Perhaps eventually. A great deal depends on whether the other man lives or dies. He is not the Earl and has not the same protections from the law."

"Even an earl cannot expect to murder somebody and evade justice. What shall you do?"

"The only thing I can do. Produce my own heir."

Kitty felt a stab to her insides at that proclamation. Of course, she had always known that one day he would have to marry. The thought of Matthias with someone else was worse than knowing she had to marry Peter.

"Of course," Kitty whispered, trying not to show her inner turmoil at the soul-shattering news. She cleared her throat as it tightened so she would not do something so ill-timed as cry. "Then we must clear up the misconception of our betrothal." She could not look at his face.

The silence between them grew uncomfortable and it was all she could do not to fidget. She should have left the room after his words, but she felt stuck to the chair.

When she could stand it no longer, she tried to sneak a glance at him. Perhaps he been distracted by thoughts of Henry... Matthias was watching her.

"I do not feel inclined to do that," he replied. "Not until I am convinced we would not suit."

Kitty wanted nothing more than to be married to Matthias, yet she knew what it was to endure a marriage without affection. "I do not wish for a marriage of convenience, my lord."

"'Tis not what I am proposing, Kitty."

Her breath hitched.

"I want a real marriage and I intend to convince you."

"But I am now your servant. My hands are red and roughened with work. I eat at the servants' table!"

"Not by my choice! You know how I feel about that charade!" he replied angrily.

"My livelihood is hardly a charade, my lord." She rose to leave.

"We are not done with discussing this, Kitty," Matthias said, trying to scramble to his feet.

"Do not stand on my account." She waved him down again, feeling guilty and frustrated by his stubbornness.

"You will always be a lady to me."

She shook her head and hurried from the room. There was no point in arguing anymore.

CHAPTER 12

*M*atthias watched Kitty leave and wondered how he had managed to bungle everything. He had been making progress, then somehow the conversation had turned in entirely the wrong direction and he had lost the little ground he had gained.

For a moment, he had thought there was a spark left, but now? Perhaps he had imagined it. Still, he could not give up. He wanted Kitty and he had no desire to go to London and pick a different bride. He scoffed at the idea. As if he could go to London and woo someone without even knowing what he would be offering her. Would he be a cripple for life? He honestly did not know.

He wished he had someone to advise him. Yet he did not know of many females he could pose those kinds of questions to. If only Waverley and Elliot were nearby with their wives, but he could hardly write to them and request such things! His old, trusted housekeeper was gone and he scarcely knew the new butler. Hornsby, bless him, had no more finesse for wooing a lady than Matthias did.

Hayes came in to remove the tea tray. "Is there anything else you will be needing, my lord?"

"No. Well, perhaps there is, Hayes. Will you close the door?"

The butler did not bat an eye at the odd request. The door closed without so much as a click and the butler stood before him to attention.

"Hayes, I realize you were not here when I was a youth, so you will not be aware, I expect, that Mrs. Gordon was also brought up here, as my father's ward."

"Yes, my lord."

"What I need is your help. She insists on pretending she is a house-keeper, but what I wish for her to be is my wife."

Matthias saw a brief flicker of surprise cross the otherwise stoic butler's expression. "Very good, my lord."

"However, I might need some assistance in convincing her. Might that be possible?"

"You wish for my help, my lord?"

"I had thought, perhaps, we could convince her that she is not suited to being a housekeeper."

"Forgive me, my lord, but Mrs. Gordon has shown herself to be quite competent. Even the servants who were very wary at first now respect her abilities. Why, she is not above polishing floors or helping in the kitchen when needed. She does not put on airs. It will be diffi-cult to convince her to your viewpoint, but I can certainly discourage the household from letting her help."

"And if, perhaps, the servants could be discreetly informed she is my betrothed and treated as the lady of the house?"

"I will certainly inform them, my lord."

"Thank you, Hayes."

"If I might add…" The butler coughed into his hand. "It would help if you could summon a chaperone."

Matthias closed his eyes. "Yes, you are correct. I will try to think of someone."

Hayes bowed and left the room.

"I am quite certain that horse has already escaped the stable, but if propriety is what they want, propriety is what they will get," Matthias muttered aloud after the door had closed.

He hoisted himself from the couch and settled his crutches in place before hobbling to his study. There he wrote two letters, letting his pride fly out of the window. They would probably tease him unmercifully but he knew they would come. He franked the letters and called for Hayes to have them delivered at once before settling into some estate business. He had a campaign to launch.

~

MATTHIAS FELL ASLEEP, having worked day and night to exhaustion. He had chosen to take his perturbation out on his leg and had been furiously exercising it and could even now put a small amount of weight on it without debilitating pain. He had scarcely touched the brandy, but there was an unexpected consequence of sobriety—nightmares. He'd had no more than one glass of brandy each evening, but it was not enough to put him into a deep sleep.

It seemed, as soon as he closed his eyes, he was immediately transported back to that awful day: the air thick with damp, smoke and heat; the ground covered with dead and wounded, and the small amount of earth exposed was mud. They had been fighting all day and he knew they could not go on much longer. The few of them who had survived were on the verge of collapse.

"One last charge, men!" One of the generals was shouting the rally cry. "The Prussians are on the way! We must hold the line!"

Matthias rallied his cavalry, making promises of one last charge that were probably false but failure was not an option. He raised his sword, signalling the charge, and the next thing he could remember was the warmth of his own blood oozing from his leg.

"You have been hit!" Colin shouted over the din of the guns and cannon. "Fall back into the square!"

"Not yet! We must finish this!" He urged his horse forward and continued to fight as a cuirassier headed towards James. Their swords clashed, and Matthias held the opponent with their swords locked until James recovered, turned back and finished the soldier. Once they had retreated back to the line, Matthias felt the energy pour out of him. He must have lost more blood than he thought, and the bullet was still lodged in his leg.

"Go and have that seen to," James ordered.

"Who is in command here?" Matthias asked, half jesting. He knew James was right. Colin pulled up beside him.

"Go to the sawbones. We will finish this last push," Colin said.

"That leaves you in charge," Matthias said, with a quick salute to Colin. He watched as Colin went over to direct some of the few men they had left and even saw Tobin stop to have a word with him before he scurried away with dispatches. Matthias would have loved to know what the dispatches said, but Colin had already set off. He could only pray it was good news and this hellish battle was over or nearly so. He stopped to tie off his leg so he would not lose more blood before riding to the medical tent, but looked up one last time at his battalion, only to see Colin being shot from his horse and then crushed under the weight of it.

Much though he tried to erase them, the images of Waterloo were there every time he closed his eyes to seek a reprieve from reality. They played over and over in his mind as if in slow motion. He had seen countless soldiers die, but Colin's demise he could not forget. This one was his responsibility—his fault.

He awoke drenched in sweat, disoriented and gasping for air. He reached his fingers for the glass next to his bed, grasping its girth, but paused before it reached his lips.

Sobriety was Kitty's price and he would pay it. She was one battle he could not afford to lose. A week had passed and Matthias had scarcely seen Kitty except for glimpses of her carrying out her house-keeper's duties. It was as though she had deliberately chosen to do more household tasks after their row, and the servants seemed to be on her side.

"Major?" Hornsby asked, looking around the door into his bedchamber.

"Come in, Sergeant. Don't gawk at the door."

"I went to prepare your medicines for the day, and there is none left."

Matthias realized what that meant. "None?"

"No, sir."

"Much though I hate to admit it aloud, I do believe they are helping."

"Of course they are." Hornsby did not hesitate to chastise him. "Do you want me to ask Mrs. Gordon for more?"

Matthias hesitated. "No, I should do it." He would have to admit he had been secretly using them. "Help me dress."

"You could do to spruce up a little. Maybe some face paint from one of the girls would do the trick."

"What is that supposed to mean?"

"You're looking a little whey-faced this morning. Thought you wanted to woo her?" he said as he began to shave Matthias.

"I have not been sleeping well," Matthias grumbled.

"Do you want to talk about it?" Hornsby goaded.

"No, I do not wish to talk about it."

Hornsby handed him his clothes one at a time without saying another word. Matthias almost laughed at the batman's surliness, but he was too worried about his appearance. Had he ever worried about his appearance before?

Once his toilette was complete, Hornsby left, and Matthias hobbled over to the mirror. What was it ladies did? They pinched their cheeks to bring colour to them, did they not? He supposed it could not hurt and then felt ridiculous. He cursed his vanity and then went to find Kitty.

He was exhausted by the time he found her. It was as though she had heard him coming and avoided him. But he had not been one of Wellington's finest scouts for nothing.

She was sitting in his mother's garden, resting on a bench while looking off into the distance. She was such a beautiful picture of serenity in that moment, he could envision a portrait of the scene hanging in his private chambers. Perhaps one day he would earn the right to that.

He moved forward, determined to be humble.

He could tell the moment he disturbed her peace. She stood up like a servant would in the master's presence. He was immediately annoyed and had to repress his anger. "Please sit down."

She cautiously resumed her seat. "Is something amiss, my lord?"

Matthias forced himself to smile. "No, quite the contrary. Your herbs seem to be working well and I have come to ask for more."

When what he had said registered on her face, her delight was worth the price of humility.

"Do you mean it?"

"I have never been one for false flattery, you know that."

"This is such a relief. Does it mean you do not require spirits now?"

"Not as much," he conceded.

"That is something, is it not? I can bring the herbs to you. I have some prepared in the still-room. I thought Hornsby knew that," she said, standing up again.

Matthias followed her and smiled. Perhaps the servants were trying to help more than he knew. Heaven knew, he needed any excuse to speak with Kitty.

"By the way, I have invited some guests. I expect them to arrive any day now."

She spun back around and looked horrified. "How many?"

"I am not certain. Perhaps four?"

"My lord, I need to make certain rooms are prepared for them." She did not hide the exasperation from her voice. Matthias bit back a smile.

"Kitty, these are not guests you need to worry about. In fact, you are well acquainted with some of them."

He could see the concern on her face. "Who?" she whispered.

"Why, Waverley and Elliot, and hopefully their wives."

"You have invited a duke and duchess and have but now thought to tell me?"

Her steps lengthened as she hurried back to the house and Matthias could not keep up. She stopped as if she remembered her initial errand. "The herbs are on the shelf in the store room," she called before rushing away.

"I have once more lost any ground I may have gained," he muttered to himself in frustration.

~

KITTY HURRIED BACK to the house, her mind in a whirl with everything that needed to be done. Had Matthias deliberately put her in a position to fail? She hated to think so, but was it not just like a gentleman not to consider what would need to be done to ensure rooms were prepared and adequate meals were sent to the table for so many people?

She began in the kitchen with the cook, almost breathless by the time she entered that door.

"Good day, Mrs. Gordon," Cook greeted her.

"His lordship has just informed me we are to have several distinguished guests, perhaps as soon as today."

"Oh, yes, ma'am. A Duke and Duchess, I hear, and the distinguished Captain Elliot and his bride. I have prepared several of the master's favourites for the occasion."

"You were aware of this visit?" Kitty asked with disbelief.

"Indeed. His lordship told me a sennight ago so I had time to send to London for provisions if necessary."

Matthias hobbled in through the door just as Kitty heard this revelation. She felt a twinge of guilt at having left him behind, but that was swiftly erased by his omitting to inform her of the impending house party. His sin was decidedly greater than hers. She marched over to the still-room and took the cordial and herbs he needed from a shelf. He followed her inside and the room suddenly felt too small, as she imagined one of the large Tower animals must feel, locked in a cage. Quickly, she moved to place the jars in his hands but he grasped hers instead, enclosing them in his larger ones.

She was so surprised, for a moment she forgot she was angry.

"I did not mean to distress you, Kitty."

"But you undermine my position by going behind my back."

She could see the indecision on his face. "I assure you, that is not what I was doing. I thought you would be pleased to see our old acquaintances. I wish you to be my guest, not my housekeeper, while they are here."

"No," she said emphatically. "Why pretend I am something I am not? They will know eventually, anyway."

"I still mean to convince you to let me help you. It will hurt them very much to know you refused to seek their assistance when you needed it."

Kitty wrenched her hands out of his grasp. "I am not their responsibility, nor yours."

"Please, Kitty. Do this for me, at least until they are gone."

"Regardless of what you think, I have been performing various tasks here, and having guests of that stature will require even more work of the other servants. You burden them by keeping me away from my duties."

Matthias smiled and his eyes crinkled at the corners. "Give me a modicum of credit. I have brought in extra help for the occasion, and Dunford's sister arrived yesterday to take over your duties."

"You are replacing me? How could you?"

"I could, because I care about you. I want you to take your rightful place and enjoy our guests!"

His hands were on her shoulders and for a moment she thought he wanted to shake her. But he would never do that. Instead, he placed his forehead to hers and looked her in the eye.

"Kitty," he whispered, then placed his lips to hers.

She should not allow it, but it had been so long since she had felt any touch—let alone Matthias's—her body did not obey her mind. She leaned into him as if she were being drawn forward with a rope.

It was soft and tender, gentle and reverent. Warmth rushed through her and, for a moment, five years fell away.

There was a knock on the door. When had it been closed? Kitty jumped apart from him and struggled to catch her breath.

"Forgive me, my lord, and my lady, but a carriage is coming up the drive," Thomas said through the door.

"Thank you, Thomas. We will be there directly."

"This cannot happen again, my lord. Promise me or I will leave now," Kitty demanded.

His jaw clenched, the way it did when he did not like something. "Very well, if you will participate as my hostess while our friends are here."

It would be lovely to see them again on the same footing, but she did not want to give in so easily. If she gave in now, he would continue to find ways to undermine her.

"Shall we?" Matthias offered her his arm, though it was more for formality with him still using the crutches.

"You leave me little choice." Reluctantly, she took his arm, her pulse still beating fast from the kiss.

"The choice is always yours, but this time I want you to choose me."

With that statement, he opened the door and almost pulled her through it, not leaving her any time to respond. Choose him this time? What an unfair accusation to make—as if she had had any choice before—and at a time when she could not argue with him. Every one of the kitchen servants, Cook included, had paused in their labours and were looking upon the two of them with curiosity.

Reluctantly, Kitty turned her attention to the guests. The new arrivals were Captain Elliot and his strikingly beautiful wife, who had the most glorious red hair. Kitty had been at their wedding, but at the time she had been barely surviving and had been trying to hide her exhaustion and hunger.

"Kitty, is that you?" Elliot asked with his devastating, darkly handsome smile. He came over to greet her, arms outstretched. "I am so glad to find you here. Do you remember my wife, Lady Amelia?"

The exquisite woman held out her arms and came straight towards Kitty. "Amelia will do very well. I am so pleased to be able to know you better. I was barely able to exchange a word with you at our wedding."

"It was lovely and you had many, many people to speak with." Kitty's wedding had been nothing like it. It had been small and impersonal, with two witnesses and the Army chaplain. "Do you wish to be shown to your chambers to refresh yourselves or would you care for some tea?" she asked, not certain whether she was enquiring as a housekeeper or hostess.

"Tea would be lovely," Lady Amelia said, and they walked on through to the drawing room. A room done in ivory with gilt, it had been decorated to Lady Thackeray's style and untouched since her death. Lady Amelia chose one of four Bergère armchairs situated about a small table which stood in front of a large marble fireplace, the latter carved with the Landry family crest. It was very quaint. The ladies sat down and the gentlemen followed.

In hot pursuit with refreshments were Hayes and Dunford's sister, apparently. Kitty tried not to be hurt by her own replacement or the woman's efficiency. The new arrival was an older woman with a severe bun, and was allowed to wear an apron and cap, and look like a proper housekeeper. Kitty cast a look of irritation at Matthias, who grinned sheepishly at her.

Kitty realized they were waiting for her to do the honours. Matthias gave her a discreet nod and she poured tea for the ladies and coffee for the gentlemen.

"I assume Waverley will be joining us?"

"He should be returning from Ireland by now. He went to attend Tobin's wedding," Captain Elliot answered. "Tobin seems to have mostly recovered. He was injured in a blast that killed Bridget's brother."

"We were unable to go because I did not think I could make the sea crossing just now," Lady Amelia confessed, patting her stomach to indicate her delicate condition.

"Congratulations, my lady," Kitty said. It was hard not to feel some sadness that she had never been blessed with children, and she would not have the opportunity if she remained a housekeeper.

"Who did Tobin find to put up with him?" Matthias asked.

"He actually married the nurse who saved your leg. General Murphy's daughter."

"Then he is wiser than I gave him credit for," Matthias remarked with a chuckle. "It will be nice to thank her in person, one day. And

119

what of James? I sent a letter to him as well, but did not receive a response."

"He mentioned venturing to Scotland, I believe,"

"Something dire must have happened for him to go home."

"James is Scottish?" Kitty asked, surprised.

"He hides it well unless it is convenient to use his brogue to charm the ladies." They all laughed. Then, sobering, Philip lowered his cup. "He went to accompany the body and inform Colin's family in person."

"I should have been with him," Matthias said and swallowed hard. Kitty knew he felt responsible.

"Colin would say it hardly changes anything and your energy would be better spent in mending yourself."

Matthias smiled half-heartedly. "Yes, he would have done."

"Tell me, Kitty, how did you find your way back to the Close?" Philip asked, obviously changing the subject so Matthias could compose himself.

She saw Matthias look at her with a warning, but she decided she would rather be honest. The pretence would be difficult to maintain. She took a deep breath. "I came here with hopes of being the new housekeeper when Mrs. Harlow retired. I grew tired of London and thought I might as well return to where I was comfortable." She opened her mouth to continue but Matthias forestalled her.

"Instead, I am attempting to convince her to be my wife."

"How wonderful!" Lady Amelia exclaimed.

"I am not succeeding so far," Matthias answered frankly, surprising Kitty.

"Oh dear," Lady Amelia said.

"Please do not let it make you uncomfortable," Kitty reassured her. "We are still friends. I simply do not wish for another marriage of convenience. I am perfectly happy to keep house for him."

Matthias shook his head. "Please help me talk some sense into her!"

Kitty could see they did not know what to do. "Would you care for more coffee or tea?" she asked.

"I think I would like to rest a little before dinner," Lady Amelia confessed.

"Then I would be happy to show you to your apartments." She cast a defiant look at Matthias before leading her ladyship from the room. Kitty had a feeling this was going to be a very long house party—and not all the guests had yet arrived.

CHAPTER 13

"Would you care to explain what that was about?" Philip asked as the ladies left the room.

"I wish I knew," Matthias said. "Let us move to my study where we may have a proper drink."

He lifted himself on to his good leg, put his crutches in place and began walking across the room.

"Is there room for a third?" a deep voice asked from the doorway.

"Waverley! I did not hear you arrive. Come join us," Matthias said, making his way to greet the Duke, and fellow member of the brethren.

"We slipped in when everyone's back was turned. Meg is settling our daughter upstairs with her nurse."

"You are very welcome. I am relieved to have you both here," Matthias said earnestly.

"You are moving quite well on those," Waverley remarked. How is the leg?"

"I can put some weight on it now. The doctor believes the bone was broken so I must stomach the splint a while longer before we know for certain."

"At least there is hope and you can move about," the Duke offered.

"We were not certain, when we left you here, if you would survive the fever."

Matthias stopped at the French cupboard commissioned by his grandfather and began to pour them a drink. He did not want to think of what might have been. Philip came over and took the glasses to their chairs.

"I know everyone was not so fortunate as I," Matthias reflected, once they were settled.

"But it doesn't lessen the blow." Philip spoke from experience. "Now, what is going on with Kitty? Your letter was a bit…vague."

"Kitty would rather do menial work than live here as a lady." He paused and decided to be fully open with his friends. "She has refused me twice."

"I beg your pardon? Why?" Philip asked, taken aback.

"I have asked myself that question continuously. I must seek a wife, and I cannot imagine anyone else. She has no other prospects. I can only think there is some aversion to me."

"Peter was never secretive that theirs was not a love-match, but I thought they were comfortable. Could something have happened?" Waverley asked.

"Not that I am aware of. That is why I have called everyone here; for advice and, frankly, to force her from the ridiculous notion of being my housekeeper."

Philip frowned. "Why is it ridiculous?" He held out his hands in an explanatory gesture. "I understand, knowing your relationship with her, that you do not wish to see her in service, but is it truly so awful for her, if it is what she wishes?"

"She should have been my wife!" Matthias slammed his hand down on the arm of his chair. "She returned here half-starved and penniless, according to Hayes. This was her last resort."

Waverley creased his brow. "She should have come to us. That was why we established the trust."

"Aye," Matthias said, downing the contents of his glass. It hurt deeply that she had not come to him. Even with all that had passed, she had preferred to live in starvation. "I need to ascertain why."

"She mentioned not wishing for another marriage of convenience," Philip remarked, as if he was recalling her earlier words.

Matthias needed to pace about, for it helped him to think. He desperately needed his leg to heal. Instead, he had to settle for tapping his foot.

"Is there some other history with you and Kitty?" Philip was an astute interrogator.

Matthias had not known the tables would be turned on him. He sighed heavily. "I suppose there is no sense in hiding it... if it will help her to see that I am not operating out of some misguided sense of duty or pity."

Waverley and Philip waited for him to gather his thoughts.

"Kitty and I were brought up almost as brother and sister. She was a wee bit of a thing when she was orphaned. Her mother was my mother's dearest cousin and so she took Kitty in and brought her up like her own daughter."

The two just listened, taking occasional sips of their brandy.

"My mother died too young. Kitty had no one else and followed Peter and I around like a lost kitten. I thought of her as a friend and a sister, I believe, but then she changed—I changed."

Philip had a knowing look in his eyes.

"The last summer I was down from university, she had grown from a girl into a woman. I was infatuated, of course, but it was more than that."

"You cared about her," Waverley observed.

"Naturally. I was not toying with her affections—I was in earnest." Matthias looked out of the window, that horrible day still fresh in his mind as if it had just happened. "I was head over heels, as they say. After the Midsummer ball, Kitty and I stayed out by the lake until dawn. We talked, we kissed, we made promises... and lost track of time. Notwithstanding the hour, my father was waiting for us when we tried to sneak back inside."

"What happened?" Philip asked.

"I was sent to my room, and by the next morning, Kitty was gone.

He cast her from the house. Instead of blaming me, he thought she was scheming to be a future countess."

Philip remained quiet. Matthias had never told any of the brethren.

"She ran to Peter, who had already purchased his commission and left for the Peninsula. Angry at my father, I purchased my own and followed, but I was too late."

"You still love her," Waverley remarked.

"I never stopped. I simply cannot marry someone else."

Philip whistled softly.

"How do you think we can help?"

"I have no idea, it was why I called the council of the brethren," he said with some embarrassment. "I am desperate."

"I definitely am of the opinion the ladies will be of more help than we will. They have a sixth sense about these things," Waverley remarked.

"Kitty cared for you then, do you think she still does? Other than in the brotherly way, I mean," Philip amended.

"At times, I think maybe yes, but then in the dark of night when I cannot sleep, my thoughts convince me otherwise."

"Sleepless thoughts are the devil's tool," Philip muttered.

Matthias could not argue with that. Those and nightmares both, he mused. It was why he drank so much. He did not know which thoughts were worse: the conscious ones or the unconscious.

"Why not try to recreate what you had before? Remind her of your lost love?" Waverley suggested.

Matthias snorted. "We danced the night away at the Midsummer ball."

"Perhaps, one day, you will dance again, but not in the next fortnight," the Duke agreed.

They all quieted, trying to think.

"We must find ways to put you together," Philip remarked.

"We have been together these past weeks, but there has been a constant strain between us over the matter of her being a servant.

Word has spread to the village, naturally, and Sir Nigel came here to force my hand because his good name was being sullied."

"Beau-Nasty Nigel?" Waverley asked. "That was his nickname at school, if I remember rightly. I gather he has not improved since his youth."

"Not one bit."

"I hope you gave him a proper set-down and booted him out of the door."

"Certainly I did, since I blame him for causing Kitty the necessity of seeking work. If he had taken her in from the beginning, as was proper, she would not be in this situation. However, he has done something that I might use to my advantage."

"I cannot imagine what that might be," Waverley scoffed.

"He told the entire village we were betrothed."

"Does Kitty know this?" Philip asked.

"Yes, and I told her I was not inclined to inform them otherwise. I made it clear to her I mean to change her mind. I only wish I knew how."

～

KITTY'S MIND was still reeling from the fact that they were to have guests, and now there were two couples plus a child to be entertained. Worse still, every time she thought to do something, one of the maids or Dunford had already seen to it. Kitty no longer felt like a lady, and would rather be the housekeeper, especially in the presence of ladies such as the Duchess of Waverley and Lady Amelia. Even as the Earl's ward, she had never aspired to such heights. How did Matthias expect her to pretend to be one of them? It was laughable. Yes, she had socialized with the other ladies while following the drum, but that was an entirely different matter. She would much rather be downstairs with the gentlemen than sitting with the ladies... except she was no longer the Mrs. Gordon they had known.

She changed into a clean gown for dinner, but she had nothing stylish to wear. The dove grey kerseymere was the nicest thing she had. "It serves Matthias right," she grumbled as she brushed out her hair to pin it up. Did he not realize how his demand would humiliate her?

"Of course he does not," she grumbled. He thought he was doing her a good turn.

If only she did not love him so much and had had the strength to walk away. But he was her weakness and she would stay as long as she could. If this situation continued, it would not be for long.

There was a knock on the door. Kitty frowned. No one ever knocked on her door. She stood up and walked over to open it, only to find one of the parlour maids standing there, her arms full of gowns wrapped in tissue.

"Do you need help, Millie? Are these some of the ladies' gowns?"

Kitty had to step aside as Millie came into the room and placed her burden on the bed. "No, ma'am. I was told that these are for you. They were sent from London. I am also to act as your maid, if it pleases you."

Kitty was speechless while she attempted to assimilate what the girl had said.

The maid was already setting aside the layers of protective fabric and hanging the gowns from every available position. "There is not much time before dinner. I hope there is one which will not need pressing."

Kitty blinked a few times as she watched in astonishment. She had never owned anything so fine even when she was in the Earl's good graces. She had scarcely been out of the schoolroom when she was cast out as a traitor. Despite her protestations, she could not help but walk over and lovingly finger the luxurious material.

"Cor, Mrs. Gordon," Millie said. "Were you really brought up here as a lady?"

Kitty found her voice. "I was, but that was a long, long time ago."

Millie smiled somewhat adoringly. "My sister said so, but I did not believe her." The dinner gong sounded below. "We should hurry, ma'am."

"I should not accept these," Kitty said, knowing Matthias had plotted against her. It would be no more proper to accept these than it was to be living in his home as an unmarried lady. Everything was so wrong and convoluted that she no longer knew what was right and proper.

"Millie, please return these to his lordship." It would serve him right, she thought waspishly, if she arrived in her housekeeper's dress.

Millie looked uncomfortable and was nervously stepping from side to side.

"His lordship told me you would argue and that I was not to take no for an answer." Her lips began to tremble.

"I would never have thought he would stoop to using the parlour maid against me." She closed her eyes. "How can I go back to my duties after this?"

"But you won't, ma'am. You are to become the Countess."

Kitty wanted to argue, but she had promised Matthias, and this young girl would feel a failure.

"Very well, Millie. Which one do you think?"

The girl's face broke out in a smile. "Oh, this one, ma'am. It matches your eyes perfectly." She was pointing to a copper-coloured silk in the latest fashion, with a high waist and capped sleeves trimmed in gold braid.

As the silk touched her skin, Kitty could have cried. It had been years since anything so soft and delicate had been against her skin.

The maid laced her up from behind and turned Kitty around to look in the glass. "You look like a princess! May I place a few curls in your hair? I've been practising on my sister."

In for a penny, in for a pound, Kitty sighed to herself. "I daresay we have time for a few."

Half an hour later, she was ready and could no longer delay going down to dinner. As hostess, she should be there to greet the guests when they arrived downstairs.

She was surprised to find she was the first one down. The drawing room held the stamp of Lady Thackeray more than any other room in the house, save her chambers, and Kitty had sneaked into this room many times after her death to sit on her favourite chair and snuggle up for a weep.

It was as if she could still feel her presence in this room, and she was comforted by that fact as, without conscious thought, she stood next to her ladyship's chair, fingering the floral designs in the damask.

"I still miss her too," a deep voice said from across the room.

"Your lordship! I did not see you there." She spun about to see him attired in evening dress, freshly shaven and more handsome than any man had a right to be, with his tawny hair and skin bronzed like a kiss of sun.

"I should have said something, but I did not wish to disturb your memories. And I was also admiring you. You look beautiful, Kitty. Thank you for wearing the gown. If I am honest, I thought you would refuse it."

"I wanted to, but you used little Millie against me."

"I learned how to strategize from the best," he answered with a charming grin.

He moved towards her on his crutches and she stood as still as a statue. This was what concerned her most. A charming Matthias was irresistible. The angry, hurt Matthias was easier to bear. She did not know how to behave or guard her feelings in this moment.

The touch of his hand to her arm made her almost jump out of her skin. It was like a bolt of lightning which set her on fire and had the power to destroy everything in its path.

"Please do not do that," she whispered.

"Is my touch repulsive to you? Earlier, I thought it might not be unwelcome."

She could hear the uncertainty in his voice and she could not bring herself to respond as she ought. "No." Her breath caught on the word as he gently trailed his fingers down the skin of her arm. Her senses were heightened and her breathing felt rushed. How she wished this were real, but how could she trust it? It was not that she did not believe he would marry her, but she did not think he could love her as she loved him. Why, then, was he doing this? She could not think sensibly when he touched her like that and it was only a small, simple touch of his fingers on her arm. Did he realize what that was doing to her?

Distantly, in her mind, she was aware of footsteps approaching and she pulled her arm away without reprimand. She did not want to attach more importance to it than was warranted. How easy it would be to allow Matthias's advances but once the newness wore off, she would be hurt again. The wounds from the first time had barely healed, and she did not want them reopened.

Thankfully, there was little time for more private conversation, although she detected hurt in his eyes. "Kitty, don't withdraw from me, that is all I ask. Open yourself to the possibility of our marriage."

She watched as he struggled to walk over to greet his friends. What must they think of her pretending to be his hostess? She did not think the gentlemen would judge her harshly; they had known her before. The ladies, however, how would they feel? The two were sisters and together their beauty could have turned the armies of Europe into drivelling fools. Kitty smiled, but felt very intimidated.

They walked towards her, and she was grateful for her gown. Perhaps Matthias had been correct about the gown, but could he not see that the rest was impossible—how much harder this would make things when his friends left? She was unable to continue her painful questions, as the ladies approached. Kitty had unknowingly stayed in her spot by the chair.

She moved forward and curtsied. "Good evening, your Grace, my lady."

"Good evening, but we must dispense with the formality, if you please," the Duchess said kindly. "Among friends, I am Meg, and my sister is Amelia."

The Duke brought glasses of sherry for each of them—something Kitty should have thought to do, she chastised herself.

"Thank you, your Grace." She dropped into a curtsy. Waverley had been Peter's commanding officer and had been next to him when he was killed. He had spent many an hour at their tent or table during the various campaigns.

"There will be none of that, Kitty." He reached forward and pulled her into a hug. "Now, what is this I hear of you trying to be a housekeeper?"

"Not you, too," she chided as she pulled away.

"Of course I, too."

It was ironic that, as an army wife, she had spent hours doing very much what a housekeeper did, but here it was considered beneath her.

He led her away from the others to the far side of the room. "Just because Nigel Gordon is a pompous spendthrift does not mean all of us are. We established a Trust for you after Peter's death but assumed Gordon was looking after you. Then you hurried away after Philip's wedding."

Kitty could not believe what she was hearing.

"You do not need to marry or be a housekeeper, my dear. You are free to do as you wish."

Kitty blinked back tears.

"We will discuss the details at length later, but I hope it will remove a weight from your shoulders and allow you to enjoy our company."

CHAPTER 14

*M*atthias watched anxiously from the other side of the room, trying to listen with one ear to Philip and with the other to what Waverley was saying.

"I just said, 'pigs fly,' and 'Prinny was frugal,' and you heard not a single word," Philip said with amusement.

The words registered a minute too late. "I am sorry, old friend. I am a little distracted at the moment."

"He will not say anything to harm your case," Philip commented knowingly.

Matthias cast a doubtful look at Philip. "I overheard him say something about the Trust."

"Yes, the one we all contributed to after Peter's death for if she ever had need of it. It should be a nice settlement for her by now."

"I had forgotten about it," Matthias admitted, "but if she had only asked one of us, we would have given her anything she required."

"Don't worry. I do believe this will work in your favour."

"How can you say that? She will have no need of me at all if she has an independence!" he said with fervour, although trying not to shout.

"Think about it. If she had accepted you before, there would always be doubt in both of your minds as to why. Now, you may woo her freely for the right reasons."

Matthias thoughtfully refilled his glass. "I hope you are correct."

"I usually am," he said dryly. "And I also hope you do not drink this steadily all evening."

"When needs must," Matthias admitted. "But Kitty does not like it."

"She understands your pain?"

"The physical part."

Philip studied him rather too closely. "Nightmares? The ones which we pretend do not exist?"

Matthias gave a curt nod. "Are you immune to them?"

"Not entirely, but talking to Amelia when they occur has lessened them a great deal."

"She does not feel burdened by them?" Matthias was unconvinced.

"Amelia had her own traumatic experiences whilst in France, so she understands more than most, but Kitty also experienced army life and you might find that speaking of it helps you both."

"I will consider it, if she ever allows me close enough," he answered, though burdening her further was the last thing he wished to do.

"She looks beautiful," Philip said, regarding Kitty where she stood speaking to the Duke.

"Like the Kitty I knew before, except fully blossomed into a woman."

The ladies had intervened and were now speaking with Kitty alone. Waverley was walking back towards them.

"Do I need to call you out now?" Matthias asked sardonically.

"I certainly have not been lecturing to her, but I have given her a few options to consider.

Matthias relaxed a little. "I would expect nothing less. I want what is best for her, of course, but selfishly, I hope it is me."

Matthias was grateful by the time Hayes came in to announce dinner. It was still difficult to stand for long periods of time and he was not so humble that he did not mind falling in a pile on the floor in front of his friends.

Dinner was an intimate affair, with there only being six of them. The table had been shortened as much as was possible to accommodate them, and Matthias had defied convention by having Kitty seated at his side. His opportunities to enjoy her company were small, and even if she was obligated to speak with him, he hoped he could begin to soften her towards his proposal.

After they were seated and the turtle was served along with some dilled cucumbers and eggs crocette, Lady Amelia broke convention and spoke across the table to Kitty. Lady Amelia and her sister appeared to be opposite in many ways. Her sister was thin and graceful, almost ethereal in her pale beauty, and Amelia was vibrant and curvaceous, with her striking red hair and personality.

"We are all friends here, Kitty," she began, with a twinkle in her eye. "I would love to know what the gentlemen were like in camp."

Matthias, Philip and Waverley collectively groaned.

It actually brought a smile to Kitty's face and Matthias knew he had done the right thing. It had been years since he had seen that smile. It took five years of living from her face again.

"Do not speak a word, Kitty," Waverley warned. "Our friendship depends upon it."

Kitty actually laughed. "I am not afraid of you," she rejoined.

She took a sip of her wine and made a show of pretending to think. "Let me see what I can recall, but most of the funny stories were of me learning to cook and keep house," she admitted.

"But I want stories I can use against Philip," Lady Amelia said impishly. "He always seems so perfect."

The other men scoffed.

"Well, there was one time, not long after we arrived on the Peninsula, when they were all still very, very new to the army," Kitty said wistfully. "As you can imagine, I had never done any laundry, but conditions were sparse and our lodging was in tents, and I thought I would be useful. There were also no other officers' wives there and I thought to join the camp followers in their activities.

Waverley coughed. "Not all, I hope."

"I would like to see you do better," Kitty snapped playfully. He held out his hands and surrendered.

"What happened?" the Duchess asked.

"Well, if you launder things of colour with white breeches, the latter tend to turn that colour."

"Oh, dear." Lady Amelia giggled.

Kitty sighed dramatically. "I was mortified at the time, of course."

"*You* were mortified?" Philip interjected. "We were the ones who had to wear pink uniform breeches until new ones could be made for us!"

"At least the five of us and our batmen all matched. It would have been much, much worse if we had been singular," Matthias added.

"That is easy for you to say. I was called Philip Pink Pantaloons by the Colonel's staff for months," he bemoaned.

"I will have to remember that," his wife said sweetly.

"It was the thought that counted," Kitty protested, bursting into laughter.

Matthias felt light of heart for the first time since he had returned home.

"I need something about Luke," the Duchess surprised everyone by saying.

"A matter of pink breeches is not enough?" the Duke asked incredulously.

"Apparently not, if you were not given a nickname," she responded.

"No one is brave enough to call him anything," Matthias teased.

"Perhaps not to his face." Philip grinned. "But there was the one time we were bathing in the Rio Tormes, near Salamanca and Peter ran off with his clothes."

"I had forgotten about that." Matthias laughed. "He tried to blame it on an animal."

"I had no idea it was him," Waverley said with an amused smile.

"What happened?" the Duchess wanted to know.

"I had to run back to camp in the state of nature I was born in, is what happened," the Duke answered in a sarcastic tone.

"And that did not garner you a nickname?" she asked with disbelief.

"Nothing repeatable in front of ladies," Matthias drawled.

"I am certain we can supply one if you are feeling left out," Philip continued to tease good-naturedly.

"Duke of nude, perhaps?" Amelia suggested.

Waverley made a noise of disgust.

"Bare-bottomed Bear?" Philip played along.

"Oh, that is delightful!" the Duchess exclaimed.

"Breeches-less buff?" Kitty added with a giggle.

"Enough!" Waverley dropped his head into his hands.

Matthias did not care if Kitty were angry with him for his antics. He would do anything to have her back like this.

"I do not know how you managed. There were five of them and only you?" the Duchess asked Kitty.

"Yes," she agreed. "Although I was used to being with Matthias and Peter. I was more of a tomboy, getting into mischief with them, so perhaps it was harder for me to learn to be a wife than for them to be soldiers."

She looked down at her plate, evidently sad suddenly, and Matthias longed to take her in his arms for comfort. He was thinking of Peter, too, and even though Peter had been her husband, he had been Matthias's best friend. Many times Matthias had thought it would have been easier for Kitty if he had been the one to die that day.

After the covers were removed and the ladies retired to the drawing room for tea, the gentlemen relaxed with some port.

"She seems to be getting on with Meg and Amelia," Waverley remarked.

"I think this is just the tonic she needed. She has not been able to be a proper lady in some time," Matthias said reflectively.

"What is the next step in your campaign?" Philip asked.

"I thought, perhaps, a picnic by the lake. And your daughter can join us."

"Ah, appealing to her maternal instincts?"

"Hopefully yearnings," Matthias conceded. "I would love a brood of children. She used to feel the same way."

"I have heard tell of your brother's duel," Waverley said as he swirled the thick red wine around his glass. "It was Worth's heir, Lord Preston, and he was not expected to live out the week."

Matthias clenched his jaw. It was worse than he feared. He had not known who the opponent was, nor his condition. He had almost let it slip from his mind, so consumed with Kitty and his own plight as he was.

"I did not know who it was," he said quietly.

"It certainly makes your campaign with Kitty more urgent. Henry will not be able to step foot in England again so long as Worth lives," Waverley warned.

"No indeed. 'Tis why I need your help."

~

KITTY AWOKE the next morning long before most ladies of the aristocracy would. She had been used to waking up to perform her duties and she would still do what she could. It was likely there would be a few hours before she would see anyone other than servants. She felt excited, despite everything. Last night had been a pleasurable escape and, for a few hours, she had forgotten her woes. It was not quite as if she had gone back in time, because she was with friends who she had shared with Peter, and they had talked about him and remembered him fondly. It was the first time in the two years since his death that she had been able to do that... had had the luxury of doing that. Somehow it made her feel more free, as if his spirit were with her and telling her everything would be well—except she knew this was only a brief holiday from reality, and it would be all the more painful when the friends left. Nonetheless, she had promised Matthias and she might as well enjoy it.

The Duchess and Lady Amelia had not been pretentious or cold to her at all—indeed, quite the opposite. They had been kind and friendly and had put her at ease.

She dressed in one of her housekeeper's gowns that she could fasten by herself, and went downstairs to tend the garden. She smiled. Lady Thackeray had ever been the same, despite being a grand lady.

There was little to be done, unfortunately. The garden was thriving and besides weeding, most of it was out of her control. The key to a healthy garden was rain, sunshine and patience.

The still-room was in order and she had prepared enough of the herbs for Matthias's treatments for another month. Kitty did not know how to be idle anymore. She was debating taking a walk when she heard voices just on the other side of the hedge from where she kneeled beside a bed of marigolds.

"Are you sure about this?" she heard the Duke's voice ask as boots crunched along the pebbled path, one gait less even than the others.

"I need to try. Perhaps riding will strengthen my leg. Look at it, man, it is smaller than my arm!" Matthias said.

"No need to exaggerate," Philip drawled. "We will see how you do."

Matthias was going to try riding? He had lost his mind. She began to stand up, set to scold him, and then stopped herself. Who was she to protest? Two of his oldest friends were there to see him through it and they would not let him come to harm. This was the very thinking she must cease if she wanted him to allow her to stay.

Yet she could not simply walk away. Following at a discreet distance, she attempted to keep out of sight, smiling with remembrance of that day she thought she had hidden on the terrace. Hopefully, he would be too consumed with the small matter of staying on his horse to notice her.

She found a perch behind the grand old oak trees they had been used to climb as children. It was certainly wide enough to hide her. If she had been able, she would have climbed up to rest on one of the large branches, but Matthias had always boosted her up because of her lack of height. Although she could hear their voices in the distance, it was difficult to make out the entire conversation.

Grooms led out horses for the three men and she watched as Matthias handed his crutches over.

He placed his hands on the pommel and stared. "I do not know how to do this even with a mounting block."

"We will help you," Philip said. "You will do it yourself again when you are stronger."

Kitty strained to hear, but was able to fill in the mumbled words.

Matthias gave a nod. She knew what this was costing him. Why would he force himself so? She gave a little shrug to herself. Gentlemen could be so stubborn. Peter would have been the same. A day not spent on his horse was like the worst form of punishment. Mayhap this would be good for Matthias, if he succeeded.

At first, she could tell, he did not want help by his determined expression. He climbed slowly on to the mounting block and tried to pull himself over with brute strength.

He made his hips to the saddle, but could not pull his injured leg over.

"May I help?" Waverley asked.

"'Tis no good on my own," Matthias admitted.

Waving the groom away, Philip moved forward and held the horse, while Waverley gently edged Matthias's leg over the saddle.

He leaned forward, resting his head on his arms. The pain must have been excruciating. She could see his breaths were slow and deliberate.

Waverley and Elliot waited until Matthias sat back in the saddle. "You go along and ride. I think I will need to stay in the paddock today."

"We have nowhere else to be," Waverley said.

She saw Matthias open his mouth, no doubt to protest, but Philip placed a hand on Matthias's arm. "This could be any one of us. It was almost me. Let us do this for you."

"I am weaker than Irish whiskey," he said, looking fatigued after one lap around the small field. "But it feels good to be on a horse again, even if I am walking slower than I did my first time in the saddle!"

"I think you have done quite well. You have managed to stay on the horse," Philip said.

"I am sure Waverley's daughter can stay on top of the horse with more grace than I at the moment," he retorted in a self-deprecating way that made Kitty's heart clench for him. Seeing his friends here was a double-edged sword. They would support him through this, of course, but they also appeared to be whole.

"I could barely stay aboard my horse after my injury," Waverley said. Kitty had not realized he had been injured. It must have happened after Peter had died.

"I fell from mine more times than I should like to recount," Philip added. "It just takes time. You are doing the right thing by taking it slowly. If you cause further injury, you might not have the ability to sit a horse later, at all."

"I do not want to be sensible," Matthias argued. "I want to be whole so I can be the man Kitty wants."

Her breath hitched. "Is that what he thought?"

"Kitty does not care about your injuries, man," Waverley scolded.

"I had not thought so, but she keeps rejecting me soundly."

"You both lost Peter and she has suffered a great deal since his death. It will take time," Philip repeated reasonably.

"Time I do not have! There is already talk in the village and I cannot court one of my servants. You know it is not the done thing."

"This is hardly a normal situation," Waverley said. "and many have done just that."

Matthias glared at him. "We are talking of Kitty."

Waverley tilted his head in a gesture of non-committal.

"What am I to do?" Matthias's voice held a note of anguish. "I cannot force her, but I cannot marry anyone else."

Kitty gasped at his words.

"We are here to help, and there should not be talk while we are present," Waverley assured him.

"You cannot stay forever. I need to dismount, now. My leg is shaking more than last night's blancmange."

When they began to help Matthias from his bay gelding as if he were a small child, she had to turn away. He would not wish her to see him thus.

Kitty had eavesdropped without conscience, and now she would have to wonder guiltily at the meaning of the words. Warm, salty tears poured down her face. She did not understand. He did not understand. If she could only see past the shield of honour he placed around his intentions—and if only he could love her as she loved him. Why was he so determined on this marriage? Nevertheless, her heart softened and she allowed herself to hope as she hurried back to the house to ready herself to join the others at breakfast.

CHAPTER 15

*M*ounting his horse that morning had felt like a very, very small step in the right direction, yet Matthias had needed to do it, to prove something to himself if nothing else. It had been more humbling than he had anticipated, to lay himself open to his friends in such a manner, yet they understood like most people could not. It had been over a month since he had first arrived home and he was due for a visit with Dr. Beverly, but part of him was afraid of what the doctor would say. If Matthias avoided the physician, then he avoided hearing anything that would devastate him. Besides, there was little he could do with the splint immobilizing his thigh; far better to keep his attention on winning Kitty over while he still had the chance.

He had worked hard with Cook and Dunford to prepare a picnic he thought would please Kitty. Tables and chairs had been taken down to the lawn by the lake. Boats had been pulled out of the sheds and polished. A new swing had been hung by the water and all her favourite puddings he could think of—strawberries with sweet cream, blackberry tart, lemon cheesecakes and pound cake topped with fresh plum jelly—had been prepared, along with fresh fruits and the estate's elderflower wine, in addition to fried chicken, cold ham and cheese from the dairy.

The day was perfect, without yet a cloud in the sky, but since this was the south of England, it could well be a different season by late afternoon. The garden had been freshly scythed, filling the air with the pleasant aroma unique to cut grass.

He remembered one such afternoon when he had been home from university. It had been the day he had first seen her in a different light. He and Peter had just ridden into the stable yard and were walking up to the house. They were still covered in road dust but having seen the gathering by the lake, diverted to greet everyone—gentry and servants alike.

Perhaps it sounded silly, like one of Byron's poems, but suddenly he had understood Byron's sentiment as never before. He found himself reciting:

SHE WALKS IN BEAUTY, *like the night*
Of cloudless climes and starry skies;
And all that's best of dark and bright
Meet in her aspect and her eyes...

KITTY HAD BEEN STANDING TALKING to Lady Gordon, her slender frame enveloped in a sprigged muslin gown the colour of a spring meadow. The sun's rays hit her hair at just the right angle, giving her a warm glow and the sound of her laughter was brighter than any summer day.

But the moment he would never forget, the image to which he had fallen asleep, too many a night in his tent on the Peninsula, was when she had turned to see him and smiled, as though he was her favourite person in the world. For a time, he had thought he was. He wanted to be again.

He had come down to the lake before the others, wanting to ensure everything was perfect. So much depended on this picnic, but nothing could be forced. If Kitty's feelings were not there anymore, he doubted they could be rekindled.

The servants had everything under control. Dunford and Hayes were very good at their positions and he told them so. "Everything seems to be in perfect order. I hope all of you will take the time to enjoy yourselves as well."

"Why, thank you, my lord," Mrs. Dunford said, beaming from ear to ear.

"We are all cheering for you, my lord," Hayes added.

The guests arrived in a group, little Lady Frances in her father's arms. Matthias could not deny he was envious and hoped he would soon have his own child to hold like that.

His heart skipped a dozen beats when he saw Kitty. He had ordered a gown like the one he remembered, and she was wearing it today. She was now a woman with a woman's curves, but she was no less beautiful. Perhaps, if he was lucky, she would bestow one of her precious smiles on him.

"This is lovely," Lady Amelia said, spinning around. "Oh! And there are boats! Will you take me for a row later?"

"Of course," Philip answered his wife, giving her a look of endearment.

"Please tuck in and enjoy the feast Cook has prepared," Matthias encouraged, indicating the tables of food behind them.

The ladies began filling their plates, followed by the gentlemen, and he quickly realized he would not be able to carry his own plate. Suddenly, there was Kitty before him, ready to take it from him.

Despite his injury, he was determined everything should be just as it had been before. He, Kitty and Peter had sat on a blanket beneath the large beech tree from which they had hung a swing.

"Where would you like to sit, my lord?"

"The blanket," he said, without hesitation. "Will you join me?"

Her eyes met his, and he knew she understood. To his surprise, something in her demeanour seemed to have changed. Was she softening towards him?

"I think that would be lovely," she said, "if it would not be too difficult?"

"It will not be graceful, but I should very much like to. It will be like old times."

"Yes," she whispered, so softly he barely heard it.

Using the tree to his advantage, Matthias lowered himself to the blanket. There were few times as an earl when he was able to relax in such a fashion.

"Your leg appears to be healing," she observed. "A month ago, you could not have done that." She handed him his plate before joining him on the blanket, tucking her legs beneath her skirts and arranging the folds gracefully. One of the servants brought them two glasses of the elderberry wine and he took a sip, relishing the moment.

"'Tis very good this year," Kitty remarked, watching him. "I have not had any since the last time we enjoyed a picnic together."

"That is one of my best memories," he said, gazing across the lake. "Memories kept me sane on the long, lonely nights during the campaigns. Did you ever think of home?"

On the edge of his vision, he could see she was also lost in thought, looking out over the gentle ripples of water that lapped against the shore.

"Of course. I remember you and Peter racing your boats."

"I remember we both tipped over and were instantly soaking."

"Yes." She laughed. "It were no bad thing, though. You were both dirty and smelled of horses."

"Ah, and we thought no one had noticed."

"It was great entertainment. I had been sadly in need of company, then there you and Peter were to brighten my day. I only wish I had been so fortunate as to have a swim in the water too. 'Twas a devilishly warm day."

"And you were no longer a child to run wild with us."

"No."

Matthias had forgotten anyone else was there save the two of them, but he was soon brought to the present when a chubby little toddler nearly hurled herself into him.

"Oh! I do beg your pardon!" Meg exclaimed as she chased after her daughter. "She saw the swing and set off at once."

The Duchess reached for the little girl, but she giggled and evaded her mother. "The more I chase her, the more she thinks it is a game. She has just begun to walk more than a few steps."

"Do you wish for a turn on the swing, Lady Frances?" Matthias asked the toddler. She had a mass of bouncing white curls and rosy cheeks.

"Wa!" she exclaimed around the four middle fingers she was also determinedly sucking on.

Kitty rose from where she was seated on the blanket. "Here you are, Lady Frances. I will teach you the secrets of the swing."

Waverley looked on with amusement. "If the two of you do not mind entertaining her for a while, I would like to take my wife for a row on the lake."

"Of course we do not mind," Matthias said. "Although Kitty will be the one to do most of the work if she requires chasing."

Kitty already had the little girl sitting on the swing next to her, and she was giggling with glee.

"I think she can manage," the Duchess said. "If not, her nurse is eating with the servants." She indicated daintily with one gloved hand.

Pall mall, lawn checkers and horse-shoes had been set up for all to enjoy, and Matthias noted that Lady Amelia was in a contest with the footman, Thomas, while Philip looked on with amusement.

Matthias turned his attention back to Kitty. She looked so natural with Waverley's daughter... as she would with their daughter.

He slowly edged himself upright as he held on to the tree. If they began to swing very high, he would be in the way.

"I think you are safe," Kitty said when she saw him move. "Although, if Lady Frances has anything to say about it, we would reach the sky."

"Or you would be in the lake, as we used to do. Do you have her safe?" He stood behind them, balancing his weight mostly on one leg, and pushed. Little Frances squealed with delight.

"That is a sound to warm the soul," Kitty reflected, "but we might be out here for hours if she has any say in the matter."

"Eventually she will fall asleep," Matthias murmured. "The key is to outlast her."

"Or wait until her parents return."

After a while, the little one leaned against Kitty. Matthias's leg ached and throbbed, but not for the world would he have stopped this scene.

He finally began to slow the swing and Kitty pulled Frances into her arms. When the swing stopped and she stood up, she was practically in his arms.

"Is she not a delight?" She looked down at the cherub-like child, burrowed into her chest to sleep.

"We could have that, Kitty."

~

KITTY HAD BEEN SAVED by the return of the Duke and Duchess.

"I did not think she would be able to sleep with so much activity going on. You have the magic touch, Kitty," the Duchess remarked softly. "I can take her to her nurse now."

"Allow me. You enjoy yourself."

Kitty was not ready to respond to Matthias's words, but they had seemed genuine. She had known he wished for a lot of children, but war had prevented him from marrying, she thought. As she had not conceived with Peter, she was worried she might not be able to, although they certainly had not tried hard.

Matthias needed an heir now more than ever. Had he considered that she had not borne a child with Peter?

Kitty looked down at the beautiful little girl in her arms, and could not imagine anything better than having her own child to nurture. She had resolved, when Peter died, that it was not God's will for her to be a mother. Then she had become destitute, but selfishly, she still longed for a child of her own. Would that be enough to make the marriage a happy one?

Even if Matthias was marrying her for the wrong reasons, the possibility of having his children was enough to tempt her.

"You are an enchantress, Lady Frances," she whispered, kissing the child's soft, downy forehead.

The nurse came to take the child and Kitty reluctantly handed her over. She looked back and saw Matthias watching her longingly. Was she only seeing what she wanted to?

It felt as if her own objections were slowly beginning to melt away, yet she wanted to be sure. Unable to avoid their friends, she walked back to the group.

"We were considering a stroll to the orchard. The plums should be perfectly ripe by now," Matthias remarked.

"I would think, after your exertions of the day, you would be tired," she responded. Then she realized her mistake. Hopefully he would not realize she knew the full extent of his activities.

"I am not as lily-livered as that. And besides, I have been recuperating for so long, this is just what I need."

The other couples preceded them and they fell into a comfortable rhythm, Matthias surprising her with his ease on the crutches.

"You saw me this morning?" he asked unexpectedly.

"I was tending the garden," she admitted. "And the garden is some distance from the stables..." She attempted to prevaricate.

He cast a knowing look in her direction.

The wretch was going to make her confess. "Had I been there, surely you would have seen me, so poor am I at hiding."

He turned and smiled at her, looking at her in a way which sent shivers down her spine.

She forced her gaze away and kept walking, conflicting emotions churning inside her. How easy it would be to be swept away by this charming Matthias, but they were children no longer. For a moment, she allowed herself to wonder what would happen if she accepted his proposal. After going down the dangerous pathway of motherhood in her mind... if they could behave as friends once again... perhaps he could love her one day.

They reached the orchard too quickly, before she had finished her thoughts. Perhaps that was for the best, her evil genius chided, because it was difficult to think clearly in his presence.

Rows and rows of trees, heavy with fruit, went as far as the eye could see in the northern direction. There were plum trees and peach trees, and apple trees which would mature in the autumn. To the south, however, was a view of the sea.

"These, my friends, are the finest plums in England." He carefully selected one for each of them, checking the colour and softness before twisting it off the stem.

The couples wandered off to enjoy the fruit and the beautiful view, which Kitty had to admit was unparalleled in comparison with many places she had been. The orchard was full of memories of afternoons when, as children, they had romped through the trees and eaten the fruit until their stomachs felt ill. It was just another reminder of what she had once had and lost. Why, if he had not wanted to marry her then, did he wish to now? Why, after having seen beautiful ladies and connexions of the *ton*, would he be concerning himself with her, if not out of his misguided sense of duty? She still could not reconcile it, yet his behaviour the past two days said otherwise. Duty was offering marriage or providing her a home, not the friendship and affection that went along with it.

She bit into the ripe plum, savouring its sweet perfection. Some of the juice began to run down her chin and she wiped at it with her hand until Matthias caught it and kissed the juice with his lips. It was difficult not to react. This did not feel like an act of duty.

"Delicious, as I remember," he said, before pulling away and taking another bite from his own plum.

Kitty had thought this old, flirtatious Matthias no longer existed.

"Will you tell me what you are thinking, instead of remaining silent? I can see the thoughts running through your mind but I cannot interpret them."

Kitty felt herself smile. "'Twould be dangerous if you could."

"Perhaps, but one could argue it would be better to know."

"For whom?"

"For both of us. All of these unspoken questions between us would have answers."

"Perhaps. Or we might only have more," she argued.

"You are determined to lead me on a merry dance," he said in exasperation, yet there was a twinkle in his eye. He hobbled over to lean against a tree, his casual pose belying the tension she could sense in him.

"Matthias, I am not playing games with you," she said softly but seriously. "I cannot help but wonder why you persist with me?"

He blew out a breath before answering. "This is one of those moments I think I would rather you knew what I was thinking than have to say it." He laughed in a self-deprecating tone.

"You seem to have recreated much of that summer day all those years ago," she remarked. "But why?"

"Can you not bring yourself to imagine why? I have not been able to convince you with words, so I sought to recreate the best time of my life... when I thought we were in love."

Kitty's breath caught in her throat and she could tell Matthias regretted saying the words, yet he continued.

"You accused me of acting only out of honour, yet you know I am not one for silky words and flatteries."

"We were very young, Matthias."

"Was I mistaken in thinking you loved me as I loved you?" The vulnerability in his face compelled her to answer.

"No." She shook her head and could not meet his gaze. "But we were different people then. We have been forged by marriage, death and war."

"Your love has died? Will you give me no hope?"

Kitty could not believe what he was asking. Did he understand nothing? "It is because of my love that I have refused you."

"Are you saying your love for Peter prevents you from loving me?"

Kitty hesitated too long while trying to form her thoughts.

"I cannot compete with that." He shook his head and began to hobble away.

"Matthias!" She hurried to catch up with him.

He did not stop and did not look at her.

"I was wrong to think I could recreate what we had. I stupidly thought we could go back."

"Is that really what you wish for?"

"Have I not just said so?"

"I suppose so, in a roundabout way. Would you please stop so we may discuss this properly?" Kitty said in growing exasperation. This was probably the most important conversation she would ever have.

He stopped and looked at her, and the raw hurt in his face told her all she needed to know.

She stepped forward and put her arms around him, not caring who saw, although conveniently, a quick glance told her no one appeared to be nearby at that moment. She felt his tension release. Dropping one of his crutches, he pulled her close.

"Please, let this be real," he whispered in her ear.

She gave a nod against his chest but hugged him tightly.

"I realize we have changed," he admitted, his voice cracking, "but I have always loved you. Whether or not you can love me in the same way, I need you to let me protect you, if nothing more. Maybe, one day, you will even be able to love me fully too. Kitty, there is no one else I can marry when my heart belongs to you."

Her throat was so tight with emotion that she could not speak.

"I want you to bear my children."

She had to find her voice. "And if I cannot?" She looked up into his eyes, which were brimming with tears. Almost without her knowledge, her hand reached up to touch his face.

"Then we will have each other, and will have to pray that Henry manages to reform himself and that Worth's son lives. I would rather live the rest of my life with you, alone, than be surrounded by children and wishing I had done more to persuade you. Five years I've had of that hell, and believe me, I should rather trade places with Peter than go through that again."

"It is harder to be left behind, sometimes," she reflected. "I have often thought he took the easy way out."

"Please, Kitty," he pleaded. "We may take our time learning each other again once we are wed."

"I, too, could not bear to marry another. Some offered after Peter's death."

"But I never did," he said regretfully. "I did not think it was proper at the time. It seemed dishonourable to Peter."

"Though I still loved you, it would have been too soon," she agreed. Nevertheless, she reflected, it would have been nice to have known his feelings. She did not care to think of the hell she had gone through.

"I also thought you preferred Peter. It was a hard blow. I had expected you to wait for me."

"Do you not see how impossible that was? If you had heard what your father said" She eased out of his arms and shook her head. "I did not feel worthy of you. I was a 'traitor' and I would 'ruin your life.'"

Matthias cursed his father soundly. Kitty smiled faintly; she had heard far worse in camps across Europe.

"Is it possible to begin again? I know we cannot offer ourselves the same young, free spirits we were, but I think we can find happiness again, together."

"Yes. We can begin again and let our hearts be our guides."

CHAPTER 16

*M*atthias should have been open with her before, he saw that now. The joy at that one simple word caused his heart to flip inside his chest. His euphoria was inexplicable.

"Kitty." He pulled her back into his arms, ignoring the pain shooting daggers up his leg and the twitching weakness in his thigh. None of that mattered.

He cradled her head and angled his mouth over hers, allowing five years of love, heartbreak, pain and grief to flow between them and start healing. She responded in kind and returned his kiss with an intensity that set him aflame.

"To think I almost allowed you to go," he said at last when she retrieved his other crutch and gave it to him. She waited while he placed it under his arm, adjusting her step to accompany him as he began the awkward gait back to the picnic. At this very moment, he would love to be able to run and shout the news from the highest hill above the valley, but such antics would set his convalescence back weeks if not months—always supposing he did not fall into an ungraceful heap with the first step.

"Peter loved me," she said carefully, "in the manner of a sister or best friend. It was not quite impersonal, but there was no deeper feeling. Nonetheless, he was kind to me and ours was a comfortable relationship. Loving you as I do, I could not bear it if our marriage was the same."

"And because of my father's treatment of you, and my apparent rejection, you thought my offer to be the same as Peter's?"

"Precisely. Can you blame me?"

"I blame myself." At least he understood a little. Though it would take time to heal all their wounds.

"I love you too much to be merely a duty."

If she did but know the depths of his feelings, she would be afraid. "Duty is not a bad thing, Kitty. You make it sound like a tedious chore."

She let a small laugh escape her. "If the truth be known, that is probably how I think of it."

"There are times when we do things we must out of a sense of duty, I suppose, but often it is interwoven with honour, which is everything to a gentleman."

A man without honour is worse than dead, she quoted. Many evenings had been spent reading Don Quixote aloud in camp. "But can you comprehend that I want—need—to be more to my husband this time? I was duty and honour to Peter, and at the time I was grateful. I am still grateful that he saved me, since I had time to grow and mature before his death. Without that, I would not have survived afterwards."

Matthias clenched his jaw. "I still will never, ever, understand why you did not come to me. Or to one of the others."

"I had lost everything. My pride was all that was left to me and I daresay it is, to me, like duty is to you."

"I think those two words and sentiments might need to be banned from further discourse between us," he remarked as they moved slowly forward.

"Thackeray!" he heard Waverley's voice calling for him.

Matthias cursed under his breath. "We are not finished with this conversation," he said to Kitty. "Over here," he answered his friend.

Waverley appeared through the maze of trees, looking sheepish.

"Forgive my intrusion, but my man just delivered this from London. I think you should see it."

He handed over a letter and Matthias read the words he had dreaded.

WORTH'S SON DIED YESTERDAY. *The Earl is seeking vengeance. He is convinced Mr. Landry did not leave England. He has set the Runners to finding him and has put a large price on his head.*

MATTHIAS GROANED and then let out an oath.

"You will need to find him before Worth does," Waverley advised.

"Part of me thinks Henry should receive his just deserts," Matthias retorted.

"But he is your heir—not to mention what will happen if Worth drags this through the courts. The stain on the family name will last for generations."

Matthias closed his eyes. This could not be happening; not now when he had just made progress with Kitty. His brother could hang.

"I had hoped Henry was wise enough to flee to the Continent, but he must have decided to gamble on the man living. Besides, he has no funds to sustain him."

"You have had no word from him?" Waverley asked.

"No. He receives an allowance, but Dunford arranges everything with the bankers in London."

"Where could he go, then?"

"I doubt he would be in the London town house without my knowledge, and my other properties are leased."

"What about here on the estate? Have you any empty cottages he would know about?"

"The hunting lodge. I spent a few days there myself not long ago," Matthias replied.

"We should have a look. Shall I send for a carriage?"

"I suppose it is worth having a look. Why the devil did he not send word that he needed funds to escape?" Matthias questioned aloud. He had heard naught of Henry himself, only of his peccadilloes from the school.

"Perhaps because you have a house full of guests?" Kitty suggested.

"The longer he delays, the harder it will be to escape. Worth will have this estate surrounded by nightfall, if I know him at all," the Duke said as he hurried away, presumably to order a carriage. By this time they had reached the lake. Matthias sank into one of the chairs to rest his leg while they waited.

"What will you do if you find him?" Kitty asked, sitting with him.

"'Tis a fine question. He is a murderer, according to English law. If he remains here he will surely be caught and have to stand trial—and the precious house of Thackeray will forever be tarnished," he answered. "If only my father were here to see the fruits of his labour."

"And if Henry escapes?" Kitty asked, ignoring his last remark.

"There will be whispers, but it will largely be hushed up. 'Tis the way of the *ton*—at least for as long as he stays out of sight."

"Then we must find him first. Hopefully, he is aware of the danger."

"Do you think he will come here?" Matthias asked doubtfully. There was no love lost between Henry and himself, since Matthias had no tolerance for the profligate lifestyle his younger brother preferred.

"He needs money. Where else could he get it?" she asked.

"By gambling? It was what got him into this fix, and in all likelihood is why he did not leave England. He was probably trying to make money by fleecing some unsuspecting classmate."

"I still cannot believe the Henry I knew would do such a thing. Murder...gambling...I will never understand young men."

"Henry is what I cannot understand," Matthias snapped.

The Duke was approaching with Philip in the trap, which on any other day would have made Matthias laugh. At the moment he was angry. When he had finally reached a degree of conviviality with Kitty, it felt as though the world was conspiring against him. If Henry stood trial and was convicted as a murderer, he could hardly ask Kitty to marry into such disgrace.

~

KITTY WATCHED the gentlemen leave and then went back to the house. Lady Amelia and the Duchess were both in the drawing room.

"Have you heard the news?" Lady Amelia asked.

Kitty nodded. "I am finding it difficult to believe such a thing of Henry, but Matthias says he has been quite wild of late."

"We must hope they will find him before the authorities do," Meg replied. "I certainly do not condone duelling or murder, but I cannot bear the thought of anyone hanging. Both men knew precisely what they were doing when they duelled and it is a risk they took." Her expression was grave. "Not to mention the effect it has on the rest of the family—families," she went on. "Waverley is close to Worth, you know. He has been a mentor of sorts to him at times."

"I cannot understand what provoked Henry to such lengths, but Matthias said they were no longer close and Henry had not come to him for help."

"Do you think he would come here now?" Amelia asked.

"Unless he has hidden himself in a hovel in London, where else could he go? He was always fond of the Close," Kitty recalled. "He and I spent more time together, I expect, than he and Matthias did. Neither of us had any company besides each other when Matthias and Peter were away at school. There were a few other children in the village, but the Earl was not keen to allow his son to 'run about like a vagabond,' as he put it. Henry was sent away to school about the time I married Peter."

"Do you think it likely he has gone to the hunting lodge?" the Duchess asked. "Did he have any special place he would frequent?"

Kitty tried to think back. "I do not remember him going to the hunting lodge as a child. It is on the far edge of the Landry property, but not a bad ride. The Earl liked it far away to give him peace."

"There is nowhere else you think he could hide? A folly or gate-house, perhaps?"

Again, Kitty tried to think back. "Yes, indeed, there are some of those about the estate. None were really places I would choose for comfort, but Henry was used to favour one folly in particular when we played hide and seek. Perhaps I shall go and look."

"We shall come with you," Amelia declared.

"No, no. That is not necessary. Besides, you need to rest. We have already spent many hours in the sun and I know you must be tired."

"But what if he tries to harm you? All men in desperate situations, gentlemen included, tend to do irrational things," the Duchess argued.

Kitty knew that to be true. Soldiers on the battlefield sometimes lost their heads when the pain or destruction became too much to bear. "I am not afraid of Henry. He may have been wild, even as a boy, but I do believe he will listen to me—even better than he would Matthias."

The ladies looked sceptical.

"I know the grounds well and I have told you where I am going. There is plenty of time before darkness falls."

"I still think you should at least take a groom or footman," Amelia suggested, yet with a note of insistence.

"Yes, I will do that."

Kitty hurried to change into a more serviceable gown and prac-tical half-boots which were far better suited to walking. She did not know why she had not thought of the old Roman folly, but if Henry were on the estate, that was most likely where he would be. She did not wish to give specifics to the ladies because she wanted a chance to help Henry. If a large group came hunting him, she was afraid someone would give him away, but Matthias should know.

Henry might have followed the wrong path since leaving home, but she could not believe him lost to all goodness.

She did go to the stables first, to see if anyone was available to accompany her, but most were still down by the lake, cleaning up after the picnic. She debated asking the [one remaining stable-] boy to saddle a horse so she might search more quickly, but reflected it would also be harder to reach the area around the folly.

Mayhap Matthias would find Henry at the hunting lodge, she mused hopefully. Then he could offer his brother the help he needed to leave England safely. She would be careful and would make sure to be back before dusk.

She walked down the path leading away from the stables, in the opposite direction from the lake and orchards where they had been earlier. The path, while not secret, had not been well maintained and had become overgrown with brambles and undergrowth.

It would have been nigh impossible to bring a horse through this and she was glad she had forgone that mode of transport. However, she wished she had thought to bring a larger knife with which to cut branches away from the thick, thorny vines.

She was moving at a much slower pace than anticipated, she realized, as she trudged through a valley of sorts; and she still had to climb up to the old folly. Would Matthias think of this place? Kitty could not tell, yet she would not give up if there was a chance she could save Henry from the hangman's noose.

What a barbaric practice! Many poor folk were hung without fair trials and for such base reasons as stealing a piece of fruit. Although duelling was equally bad, of course. There was a reason it had been outlawed, but gentlemen still occasionally practised it to defend their honour. There was that word again.

"Bah!" she sucked in her breath when she cut her hand on a particularly sharp, long thorn. She brought her hand up to her mouth and sucked on the wound to alleviate the pain. Turning as she did so to watch the sun fall further in the sky, she willed the golden orb to stay aloft for a while longer before then beginning the final climb to her destination.

"Those poor sods who had to build such a structure," she said sympathetically, not minding her unladylike use of slang. At least she did not have to carry heavy marble on her climb.

When she caught sight of the folly at last, she stopped to catch her breath. If Henry was there, he had done an excellent job of not disturbing anything. Her heart sank with the realization that he was probably not there. It was a pity the little temple had been neglected, for it possessed a breathtaking view of the sea from its high point on the estate. She stopped to admire the sun's glorious rays casting arms over the water's seemingly endless depths.

However, the sun would soon go below the horizon and she would have to make her way back in the dark. She forced herself to look in the folly, the heavy metal door creaking on its hinges. When the spiders' webs greeted her face, suddenly she felt foolish for having adventured out on her own.

An arm came around her from behind, clasping her mouth, and then she felt the cold tip of a metal blade on her throat.

She fought to free her mouth. "Henry! 'Tis Kitty!"

"*Kitty?* You should not be here! You should have left me alone!" His voice shook with panic.

"I came to help you," she said, deliberately trying to sound calm. She could tell by his voice that he was terrified and frantic.

"You should not involve yourself, Kitty. If I have one ounce of humanity left, it is telling you to turn around and forget you knew of this place or that you saw me here."

"It is only a matter of time until they find you, Henry. We have received word Lord Worth has hired Runners and has put a price on your head. Matthias is out looking for you, to try to help you get away before Lord Worth finds you."

"He would sooner turn me in. His sense of righteousness would forbid his helping me," he spat derisively. "Preston died, you know."

"We did hear. But you are wrong, you know. Matthias does wish to help you. If you will credit him with no brotherly reason, then at least allow him to preserve the family name."

"Ah, yes. The family name. The one which was supposed to be mine, but my brother had to live and my opponent had to die. This is my fortune of late, or, rather, not fortune but luck."

The conversation was not going in the direction Kitty wanted it to. "Henry, will you please remove the knife from my throat?"

"Will you leave me here and not tell anyone?"

"How, then, am I to help you? You need food, money and transportation out of England," she said, trying to reason with him.

He laughed, in a further display of contempt, and it frightened her. For a moment, she had thought he was the old Henry, but now she was not sure. "Henry?" she asked tentatively.

CHAPTER 17

The gentlemen returned to the house. Matthias had pushed himself beyond the point of exhaustion and his leg throbbed like the devil. They had not found Henry, and he could not say whether he was relieved or disappointed. It only prolonged the inevitable, but they had to find his profligate sibling before the Earl did. Worth had a reputation for ruthlessness, and now his heir was dead by Henry's hand.

The ladies rushed to greet them, except the one he wanted to see was not with them. "Where is Kitty?" he asked as he struggled over to a chair. "Forgive me, I must sit down."

"Please go ahead," the Duchess waved him down. "We have been too anxious to sit a great deal."

Clearly sensing his friend's pain, Waverley immediately brought Matthias a glass of brandy.

"Thank you," he said with relief, then took a sip of the liquid fire. "Now, where is Kitty?"

The two ladies exchanged guilty glances. "She went to look for Henry," Amelia admitted at last.

"Alone?" he asked slowly, in too much pain to shout in the way he wanted to.

"She said she would take a groom, but she also said she would return by nightfall."

"Did she say where she was going?"

"A folly where they had been used to play as children. She mentioned it was his favourite place to hide."

Matthias narrowed his gaze in thought. "We passed the folly on our return here and there was no sign of either her or Henry."

"Oh, dear," the Duchess said, looking distressed. "This is my fault for asking her questions."

"It is hardly your fault for trying to help, my dear," Waverley remarked.

"I will go to the stables and discover which groom went with her," Philip said and slid from the room.

"May I take it you did not find Henry at the hunting lodge?" Amelia queried.

"No. There was no sign of him having been there," Waverley answered.

"Where else is there to look? London? The ports?" Amelia asked doubtfully.

"Unfortunately, with Worth having already engaged the Runners, unless Henry comes here there is little we can do."

It was not long until Philip returned from the stables. They all gazed at him with anticipation. The look on his face told Matthias what he needed to know.

"There are no horses or grooms missing."

"She went alone?" The Duchess sounded distraught.

"It appears so. The Head Groom told me they were all helping clear away the afternoon's festivities or seeing to their duties, and some had been given the evening off."

"We must mount a search for her. It is now dark and I believe she would have returned if she could have done," Matthias declared, trying to force himself from the chair.

"I do not think you are in any case to go anywhere," Waverley remarked. "She knows the estate well and it is not a cold night, thankfully."

"What if Henry has her?" Matthias argued.

"Do you think he is capable of doing her harm?" the Duchess questioned. "She said they were once close."

"I do not think he is in his right mind at the moment. When he is himself I cannot think he would hurt her, no, but he is a fugitive and has already murdered one man."

"I will go and rouse the menservants to help search," Philip said, and promptly left again.

"I will go with Philip, but you need to remain here, old friend."

"Absolutely not! No one knows the estate like I do!" Matthias protested.

"We will have grooms with us," the Duke stated flatly and pointed Matthias back to the chair. "You will only hinder us. We took the carriage roads on our way back from the hunting lodge. For certain, anywhere else we go will have to be in the saddle or on foot."

Matthias knew the Duke's reasoning was sound, but it was painful to admit he was not capable of helping his love when she was endangered. What if Henry had hurt her?

The gentlemen set off again with every able body to assist, and Matthias was left with the two ladies.

"Try not to worry," Amelia said as she brought over the decanter and refilled his glass.

"For a day that was going so well, it has certainly turned into a crushing failure," he said, raising his glass in acknowledgement of her kindness. "Much obliged."

"I suspect you will need far more than brandy before the night is through," she conceded.

"I must keep my head, but at the moment the throbbing in my leg is barring rational thinking."

"It certainly was very inconsiderate of your brother to pull such a stunt at a time like this," Amelia agreed dryly.

"Considerate would not be in Henry's vocabulary," Matthias retorted.

"Do I hear a carriage coming up the drive?" the Duchess asked.

"It is probably only some of our men setting out in various directions. It is much too late for anyone to be calling."

"My lord," Hayes said from the threshold. "Lord Worth is here to see you."

He had scarcely said the man's name when he was almost run over by Lord Worth's impulsive entry into the room.

"Thackeray! I demand to know where your scapegrace brother is! He has murdered my son and I demand satisfaction!"

"I am very sorry about Preston. I have just heard the news from Waverley." Matthias tried to convey his genuine sympathy without overly slurring the words.

"The Duke is here?" Worth turned at that moment, evidently then to see that her Grace and sister were in the room. "Forgive me. I am consumed with grief at the moment." He made a bow to the Duchess and Lady Amelia.

"Understandably so, my lord," the Duchess said in a soothing voice, inclining her head.

"Where is Waverley?" he asked, looking around the room.

"One of my servants has gone missing and he and Elliot have gone to look for her. As you can see, I am in no condition." Matthias indicated the splint on his leg.

"I heard about your injury. For your sake, I hope it heals well. From what I hear in the clubs, your brother was counting on succeeding you. 'Tis what landed him in this deep hole."

"I beg your pardon? I had a letter that he was being sent down for gambling, but are you saying his wager was that I would die?"

"It was rumoured that you had been brought back to England barely alive and were not expected to live out the week. I even heard Waverley say it was a possibility."

Matthias muttered an oath under his breath.

Worth began to pace up and down, to the imminent danger of the Axminster carpet. "Regardless of why, he lost an enormous sum to my son. When Preston allowed him a chance to win it back, he cheated— in front of a dozen witnesses."

Matthias ran a hand over his face. It was worse than he had thought. "And instead of deloping, he shot Preston?"

The Earl nodded with a look of pain etching his features. "You have not seen him?"

"I have not," Matthias answered with complete honesty. "He has not once mentioned any trouble or asked me for assistance."

Worth gave a slight nod. The dark circles under his eyes and haggard appearance were a testament to his duress. All of his purpose was now concentrated on finding Henry and making him pay.

"I hope I can count on you to give him up if he should come crawling to you for help, but warn him that I will not rest until I find him."

"Do you think he is still in England? Waverley had heard word he might have fled to the Continent."

"My men believe he remained near Oxford, waiting to see if my son would live. According to his comrades, they do not believe he had the funds to escape and they could find no one of his description having left from the ports. It only seems logical that he might flee here, being near to the Channel as the estate is."

"Knowing Henry, he would rather sully the family name than seek help from me."

"Be that as it may, he will soon know, if he does not already, that I am like a hound on a hunt. You will let me know if you find him?" he pleaded. "I only wish for justice.".

The ladies had been noticeably quiet during this exchange, which was wise. Worth was in pain and needed to have his say.

"I will certainly let you know if I hear anything that will be of use," Matthias answered non-committally. "It is growing late. May I offer you a place to stay?"

"Thank you, no. I have taken a house in Worthing. That is gracious of you though, considering," Worth remarked. "I will see myself out."

"When he first arrived, I thought he might take his anger out on you, but he was eerily calm and logical," Amelia observed as they heard the carriage depart.

"He is the same in the House. It is difficult to go against him. He never loses his head and he almost always wins."

"It is almost enough to make me sorry for your brother," the Duchess added.

～

"YOU DO NOT WANT to hurt me, Henry. The first death was an accident, and this would be cold-blooded murder." She could feel him wavering, although his breaths were ragged and his hands shook. He smelled worse than the pig sties on the home farm.

"I do not wish to kill you. You were one of the few people to be nice to me,... but I am not above using you to my advantage."

"What can I do? I told you I came here to help you," she pleaded, her voice unsteady.

"Matthias loved you and I wager he does still." His voice had changed from fear into one of cold calculation. It made her blood freeze in her veins. "Have you ever wondered why he has not married? He was still pining for you. He set off to the Peninsula hoping to stop you from marrying Peter." He scoffed derisively. "He wanted to marry you himself. He and Father had a big row about it."

"No," she argued, not wanting to think about what his words meant.

"I heard it myself. I had been the one intended for the army."

"That was many years ago, Henry." What could she say to make him put down the knife and release her? The sun had slipped beyond the edge of the sea and it would soon be full darkness. Unfortunately, it was not a full moon. She had to get away soon. Staying here all night with him...was unthinkable.

"Matthias is loyal to a fault. If he loved you then he will love you now." His voice indicated he did not consider such behaviour a virtue.

Was he completely lost, the Henry who had been her friend and playmate as a child?

"Henry, please release your hold on me. I mean you no harm."

"What would Matthias be willing to exchange for you?" He seemed to be plotting aloud.

"There is no need to make any exchanges!" she said with disgust. "He will give you what you need—but you must hurry and leave the country."

Henry released her and sank to the ground, apparently completely dejected. His moment of posturing had not been long lived.

"Matthias was to have died."

"What do you mean?"

"I had been told he was brought back and soon after died. I thought I was the Earl."

"Good heavens. Is that what you duelled over?"

"In part," he admitted. "I was indebted and his death would have been my salvation. Instead I have a bounty on my head." His tone indicated no acceptance of responsibility for having gambled or engaged in the duel.

Kitty disliked the look in his eyes even more now that she could see him. He looked much older than his one and twenty years. His eyes were bloodshot, his hair and clothing dishevelled and he wore a full, shaggy beard.

"Leave," he commanded unexpectedly.

She hesitated, now wondering if he would harm himself.

"Leave! Before I change my mind and do something you will regret!"

"I think something will be regretted regardless of whether I stay or leave." She tried to assess his state of mind. He seemed to waver between lucidity and delirium. Which was the reality?

"What will you do? I can return with food and money."

He cackled. "You have turned practical now, Kitty. Your mourning clothes make you look drab. You used to be fanciful. I used to think you were a little fairy."

For a moment, Henry had forgotten his agitation and was thinking of a better time. It did not last long, however. He turned his gaze upon her once more.

"Henry, you must do something. You cannot stay here forever."

"Why not? I have been here for some days and no one has been the wiser."

"Why not speak to Matthias? He will help you, I assure you. Moreover, Worth or his Runners will hunt you down eventually. Do you want to live like that? Always looking behind you?"

"If I were the Earl, it would be another matter altogether."

"What are you saying, Henry?" Kitty hoped she had misunderstood.

"Perhaps I shall still be the Earl." He then looked at her with such fierce intensity, she was terrified he meant it.

She turned and ran away, bursting through the old door, hurrying as fast as her feet would carry her down the hill, not stopping to protect herself from the thorny thicket. Only when she had reached the valley did she pause to catch her breath and relieve the stitch in her side.

What was she to do? She had to warn Matthias!

Once the pain subsided, she forced herself to keep going. She had passed through the worst part in the dark because she had not stopped to consider what lay ahead.

Her arms and legs were still shaking with fear, but it did not appear that Henry had chased after her. Part of her had thought he would change his mind and hold her for ransom against Matthias.

Was he up there now, plotting to kill his brother? Did he really believe he would not be prosecuted if he killed his brother in addition to Viscount Preston?

He has lost his mind—and that made him very, very dangerous. Someone had to bring him to his senses and help him get away.

Kitty passed by the orchard and then came to the path by the lake. Had it only been a few hours since she had been in that dream-like state with Matthias, when they had declared their love for each other still existed? He had wanted her before! It was as if happiness had been dangled in front of her and was about to be snatched away forever.

"Kitty?" a low voice called. "Kitty, is that you?"

She could not make out the face in the dark but it was one of the gentlemen. Relieved, she turned and walked towards the lantern and the voice.

It was Waverley. "Thank God! We have been searching for hours."

"Forgive me. I told the ladies where I was going. I thought Matthias would understand where I was."

He put his arm through hers to lead her back to the house. "Goodness, you are shaking! What happened?" He removed his coat and wrapped it about her shoulders.

"I think it would be easier if I told it once."

Waverley nodded his understanding. "Cover your ears." He whistled loudly and after a few moments, several of the servants began coming towards them.

"Mrs. Gordon is safe. Everyone can return to the house for now. Spread the word, please."

The servants acknowledged the Duke and went on their way.

They walked in silence back to the house, Kitty trying to assimilate her thoughts from the predicament they were currently in. Henry was like a fuse about to light a cannon, and time was running out to diffuse him.

Hayes opened the door for them, and his face looked shocked and relieved at the same time.

The Duchess ran out into the entrance hall. "Thank goodness you have been found!"

They walked on into the drawing room, where Matthias and Lady Amelia were waiting for them. Kitty removed her coat and handed it back to the Duke.

"Good God, Kitty! What happened to you? You look as though you have been attacked by a wild cat!" Matthias exclaimed without preamble.

She looked down to see her gown was in shreds and stained with blood. As her nerves began to settle, having reached safety, the sharp sting of her cuts began to make their presence known.

"Come," the Duchess said kindly, leading her to a settee. "Husband, do you send Hayes for some warm water, towels and salve?" she asked the Duke.

Lady Amelia rose and poured her a brandy and placed the glass between her hands.

Kitty detested spirits, but she certainly needed something to soothe her shattered nerves.

Hayes returned with the supplies and set them down next to Kitty. The Duchess began tending to her scratches.

"I can see to them myself," Kitty insisted, reaching for the towel Meg was wringing with water.

"Nonsense. Tell us what happened when you feel ready and I will take care of this."

Kitty took a sip of brandy and a warm tingle washed through her. "After you left to go to the hunting lodge, we were sitting in here talking about where else Henry might go. That is when it occurred to me that as a child, he always chose one particular place to hide."

"Meg mentioned the folly, and we checked there on our way back from the lodge," Matthias explained.

"Not that one," Kitty shook her head.

"You don't mean the old ruin at the overlook point? I have not been up there in years."

"The path was very overgrown." She indicated the cuts and scrapes all over her arms and hands, and winced as the Duchess plucked a thorn from her side.

"You should not have gone up there alone."

"There was no one to go with me. However, I did find Henry."

"I beg your pardon? I gather he would not return with you?"

Kitty shook her head. "I did not invite him to return, knowing Lord Worth is looking for him."

"Worth was just here, in fact," Matthias said baldly.

Kitty felt her eyes widen with the knowledge. "Has he gone?" she suddenly thought to whisper.

"Yes. Please continue."

"There is little else to tell. He has been there a few days and seemed disinclined to come to the house to ask for your help."

Matthias showed little reaction to the words.

171

"He was not in a good state of mind," she said, trying to think of how to explain.

"That is hardly surprising," the Duke remarked.

"What do you mean, Kitty?" Matthias understood she was trying to tell him something.

"It seems he thought he was going to be the Earl, and he thinks that, by becoming the Earl, he will solve all his problems."

Stunned silence met her statement before Waverley exclaimed, "By Jove, are you saying he means to kill Matthias?"

CHAPTER 18

$\mathcal{M}$atthias could not believe what he was hearing. Although he had no great kinship with Henry, he would not have thought his brother wished him dead.

"He told you this and then simply allowed do you to leave?"

"Yes and no," Kitty said carefully.

"I can see why you did not invite him back to the house," Philip remarked dryly.

When had he slipped into the room?

"Should we go and try to talk to him?" the Duke asked.

"He was reluctant to leave the folly," Kitty responded.

"It would be impossible for me to go there." At the moment, Matthias was not certain he could cross the room.

"Judging by Kitty's appearance, I can imagine why," the Duke commented with a rare hint of humour. "I am sure I cannot tell what possessed you to try it, Kitty."

"What do you propose we do?" She ignored the remark.

"Somehow, we have to get him out of there. It is not far to the coast—if you think we could bring a boat in to the cove," Philip suggested.

"Worth has his men watching the ports, but whether or not he will try to plant men on your land, I have no idea," Waverley said. "I believe that is going too far for his sense of decency," he added, and he knew the Earl better than Matthias and Philip.

"I believe he would," Amelia said, pondering the idea. "The gentleman who was here was not above spying, I am certain of it. He is angry and distraught, a dangerous combination."

"Besides, we need a boat," Philip put in.

"I have already arranged for one," the Duke announced.

"Of course you have," Matthias murmured, although he was grateful to have friends with such connections.

"I do not know how you will get him down. I offered to bring him food and money and he laughed," Kitty explained. "He does not seem inclined to leave England."

"He will leave if we have to bind, drug and gag him," Philip stated with calm confidence.

"It will be impossible to sneak up on him," Kitty warned. "He had a knife to my throat before I knew he was there."

"I shall kill him myself," Matthias growled. Who could want to harm Kitty?

"He did not know it was me at first," she said, as though reading his thoughts. Perhaps the fact that he was gripping the chair was some indication. "He did allow me to leave."

"But you were afraid of him." It was not a question.

"I cannot deny it. I saw some glimpses of the Henry I knew, but he is now driven by something evil."

"Kitty, I need precise directions to this folly." Philip walked into the centre of the room, looking determined. "I have a general idea, but more information would be a great help. My search took me down to the sea, yet I believe I know where he is hiding."

"Surely, you do not mean to go after him?" She did not mask her disbelief. Obviously, Kitty was unfamiliar with Philip's history as a trained operative for the army.

Philip smiled devilishly. "It will be nice to make use of my skills once again. They do me little good in retirement."

"If anyone can catch him, I would put my money on you," Matthias said. "I wish I were capable."

"I am," Waverley offered. Both Matthias and Philip looked at him sceptically. "What? Just because I was not one of Wellington's beloved scouts does not mean I cannot be cunning."

Matthias looked at Philip. "Your choice: either Waverley or Hornsby. You must have some help."

Philip's lips twitched at the comparison between the graceful Duke and the unrefined batman. He paused for effect, as though he were thinking about it.

"I am not amused, in case you were wondering," the Duke said in withering tones that made Matthias chuckle.

"We need to be in place before dawn, when he will think he is safe and try to sleep." Philip would know first-hand. He had hidden himself for a long time while on a secret operation and they had all thought him dead.

"Any supplies you need, you are welcome to... besides rope, drugs and a gag, of course." Matthias could not mask his sarcasm. He should be the one dealing with this. Instead, he was forced to rely on his brethren.

Philip gave a brief salute of acknowledgement.

"I should go, too. It would be easier than trying to draw a map. And you will not be able to follow a map in the dark," Kitty said in a low voice to Philip, but Matthias heard.

"No. You have put yourself in enough danger." Matthias never wanted Kitty to leave his sight again. Even as he looked at her now, he wanted to find Henry and tear him apart, limb by limb, for what Kitty had gone through in the name of helping the fugitive.

Kitty ignored him and turned to Philip. "I also have a chance of reasoning with him. If he realizes we are there with a means of escape, he might come on his own."

"Perhaps I should go as far as I can," Matthias wondered aloud, "so I will be available."

"No." The answer came simultaneously from a multitude of voices.

"Supposing he demands to see me?" he objected.

"Then he can leave his perch. You would be a sitting hen if he has determined you are his next victim." Philip's calm reasoning brooked no argument.

"And what about Kitty? He could make her his target!"

Why was Philip not objecting?

"She is right, Matthias," he said softly. "I will do my best to keep her from harm, but we do not have time to delay and I might not have another choice."

"I am hardly in a position to argue, am I?" Matthias spat in response.

"Trust us to do what is right," Waverley said before he and Philip left the room with their wives, having agreed to meet back there in three hours.

"It is not you I do not trust," Matthias grumbled, eyeing the brandy decanter which was unfortunately across the room. He groaned and threw his head back, alone with his thoughts.

"What can I do to help? Are you in pain?"

"I thought you had left with the others."

"No," she said, and came to kneel before him.

"Just being here helps," he said, reaching up to push a loose lock of hair from her face. Then he took her hands in his and tenderly kissed each of her cuts, one by one. "I do not want you to go. I could not bear to lose you again."

She smiled apologetically. "If there were a better way, I would not. But there were moments I was able to see the real him. I do not think he will react well to strangers."

"They are not complete strangers," he pointed out weakly.

She did not voice a reply, only looked up at him with those golden eyes that had haunted his dreams. He lifted his hands to cradle her face and placed a soft kiss on her lips.

"Promise me you will never do something like that again. When I came back and no one knew where you were…" He swallowed hard, unable to finish the thought.

"Henry must be dealt with; then we will attend to you and I."

"I love you, Kitty. I will not lose this chance to say words I should have said long ago. I never want you to doubt the strength of my affections again."

She smiled at him, a tear rolling down her cheek as her chin quivered. He smoothed it away with his thumb.

"All we can do now is look forward to the future. It is hard not to look back with regret, but we both know there is no guarantee of tomorrow."

She leaned forward into his arms and hugged him tightly. "I never thought I would be able to do this again."

"Oh, Kitty, my love. I will never let you go."

"Just try to be rid of me now," she said, with a teasing grin which he quickly replaced with another, deeper kiss.

~

KITTY HAD NOT TROUBLED to attempt sleep. Between the mixture of nervousness and anticipation and trying to reassure Matthias, sleep would have eluded her if she had tried.

At Philip's advice, she had dressed as a groom, with dark breeches, a dark coat and tall boots. At least she would be better protected from the thistles and thorns, she reflected.

Half a dozen of them met downstairs, equipped with ropes, lanterns and tools to cut away the overgrown path.

Frankly, Kitty was surprised by the number of people gathered, but she trusted Philip and the Duke. When everyone was present, they collected around Philip for directions.

"We will follow Mrs. Gordon, since she is familiar with the route. When we reach the path from the lake, there will be complete silence. Lanterns will be covered; and when the path becomes treacherous, we will clear it without making a sound. Before we begin the ascent to the folly, all of you will wait at the bottom for my signal. Does everyone understand?"

"Yes, sir," they answered solemnly.

Kitty looked at the faces of those who had been selected, and all of them had known Henry as a boy. She suspected that was deliberate. Loyal retainers were more likely to understand what was at stake.

They left in silence, Philip indicating for Kitty to lead the way, while he and the Duke followed right behind her with their lanterns.

It was not a short walk, and Kitty felt a horrible sinking feeling that worsened with each step—as though she had a large rock inside her which wanted to be free.

Encouraged by Captain Elliot and the Duke, Kitty set a good pace. Indeed, they hurried through the first part of the journey without trying to be overly quiet. Their boots made a rhythmic pattern through the various terrains of gravel, earth and grass as they proceeded, interrupted only by the occasional squawk or howl from an animal disturbed by the unusual appearance of nocturnal humans. Earthy scents, mixed with salty sea air, filled Kitty's nostrils as her breathing became heavier with exertion. When they reached the bottom of the valley before the climb to the folly, she stopped and inclined her head to Captain Elliot. He held up his hand to stop the group. They halted before him.

He gave a signal to the men and they covered their lanterns, pausing to slow and quieten their breathing while their eyes adjusted to the darkness.

"Wait here," he whispered to Kitty.

Two of the men began to quietly cut away at the path which led straight up to the folly and the other men dispersed in a semicircle, surrounding what they could. Unfortunately, with the folly sitting at the highest point of the estate, there was a steep drop down the far side of the hill on which it stood, making an approach that way nigh impossible.

Kitty waited as she had been told, but found it difficult to stand there on her own. In the dark, every movement, every sound, was heightened and she was already on tenterhooks over what was about to happen. She did not want to see Henry harmed, and she did not think he would cede peacefully to these men he hardly knew.

Even once her eyes had adjusted to the darkness, Kitty could scarcely see. How must the searching men feel? She doubted if they had been able to clear enough of the path to escape all scratches and scrapes. Occasionally, she caught sight of a shadow-like movement, but nothing she could be certain about.

They should have reached the folly by now. What was taking so long?

It was hard to be patient, not knowing what was happening. She would have thought she would have heard voices if they were negotiating Henry, but there was nothing.

The longer she stood there at the bottom of the narrow, rocky path, the more vulnerable and worried she felt. What was it about darkness and the unknown that began to erode at a normally steadfast mind? She would be a dreadful spy, because she had no patience.

She began to debate whether to go up to the folly herself. Matthias would be angry, of course, but he was not there to prevent her.

She knew they would not return to the house and leave her, but she was serving no useful purpose by staying where she was. Slowly she began to creep forward, knowing the path was just in front of her.

Every step sounded like a hammer against brick, and she stopped to see if she had been discovered, but nothing seemed to change. Once or twice, when she stepped from the path, a sharp thorn would quickly set her on the straight, but narrow, track again. As she drew closer, she stopped now and then to listen, but there was utter silence. Something was wrong. Henry should have been found by now. Either there should be voices or there should be sounds of a scuffle... but not silence.

When she reached the pinnacle, she could just make out the white marble folly, and paused while she strained to see if anything were going forward.

Cautiously, she moved closer and then closer still. Suddenly, a lantern appeared in her face, near blinding her with both flame and fright. Somehow managing not to scream, she threw her hands up in front of her face in a feeble attempt to protect herself.

"Kitty!" Philip exclaimed in a loud whisper. He drew the lantern back beneath the blanket which covered it. "We thought you might be Henry."

"No, I grew worried. You have been gone quite a while."

"We have the folly surrounded, but there is no sign of him thus far," he whispered close to her ear.

"There was no sign of him when I came earlier, either. Have you gone inside?"

"No. We were about to make the attempt when we heard you. We needed to secure the perimeter first."

"The door creaks loudly," she warned.

"Stay here unless I call for you," he warned. "I do not wish to answer to Matthias if any harm befalls you."

Kitty smiled a little to herself at the ridiculous notion, then quickly sobered again. This was no laughing matter.

She stilled, waited and then watched as the men moved forward. The door groaned loudly on its hinges as if it were angry for being disturbed in such a fashion. It opened, to be immediately followed by a sudden burst of light as lanterns were brought forth from their coverings. It was an effective disarming technique, as Kitty had just experienced.

She waited with bated breath, but nothing happened.

Philip moved inside and she could see the lantern being lifted as though he was searching the interior, shadows and flames flickering and dancing off the curved walls, and domed ceiling. There was still no sound of Henry. Without conscious thought, she moved forward, fearing the worst. She began to shake, but could not stop her forward momentum.

Philip appeared at the door. On seeing her, Waverley also approached the entrance, perhaps to stop her from seeing something horrific.

"Is he…?" Her throat choked on the word.

Philip shook his head. "Henry is not here.

"What?" she asked, rudely brushing by him to look for herself. Indeed, the folly was empty save for spiders and animal droppings. There were a few signs that he had been there—a clearing in the dust and some refuse—but he was, most definitely, gone.

"I must have scared him away... but where could he have gone?" Then realization struck her. "Matthias! He has gone after Matthias!"

Philip and Waverley looked at each other and gave a nod. Kitty did not wait for them to respond and hastened back down the path as quickly as she dared. Other footsteps followed closely behind her, lanterns now uncovered to light the way. At least this time she did not meet with as much vegetation to tear her to shreds, she thought gratefully. Once she was back on level ground, she ran as fast as her feet would carry her. The blood roared in her ears and pains in her side threatened to steal her breath yet she scarcely paid it credence. Nothing compared to how she would feel if Henry harmed Matthias.

Please God, do not let us be too late, she prayed over and over in her mind as she ran.

How stupid she had been! She knew Henry quite well enough to realize he would not have stayed hidden in the folly once he had been discovered. Yet would he truly kill his own brother?

The path seemed to grow longer instead of shorter, but she could not stop to rest.

CHAPTER 19

*M*atthias had only moved as far as the study since the others left the drawing room. Hornsby had reluctantly left him there with the decanter and a stool for his leg. It was torture, knowing his friends were attending to his business for him. Despite several glasses of brandy, he was still entirely too lucid.

He had listened as the group had gathered and set out to the folly, and he sat waiting, watching the clock tick time away in slow, rhythmic agony. Like a ship on a stormy night, his mind vacillated back and forth between wondering what was happening at the folly and remembering Kitty's sweet kisses.

His leg ached from having been on the horse earlier, then walking all over the estate. Muscles he had never known existed screamed their displeasure at him. Recklessly, he untied his splint. Thus far, he had only taken it off for minutes at a time to bathe, trying to follow Dr. Beverly's instructions perfectly. However, this felt like freedom. Muscles relaxed that had been constricted and confined. It made him think of ladies with their corsets and the suffering they put themselves through for beauty.

Gingerly, he raised his leg, bending it towards his chest with slow, shaking movements. It was an exquisite kind of pain to move the leg again. He repeated the movement two more times, up and down. Feeling bolstered by his success, he wanted to try walking—just a few steps. It was time to try. He wanted to be whole again for her. He needed to be.

Easing forward, he placed his hands on the arms of the chair, his feet on the floor, and pushed up, keeping his weight on his good leg. Once steady, he allowed his weight to distribute evenly. The blood seemed to rush to his leg, and he wondered if he should wait until Hornsby was there to catch him.

"Have courage," he muttered before moving the leg forward. It was more of a shuffle than a step. "I feel like an infant." He brought the other leg forward, and when he shifted his weight, the leg collapsed from under him and he landed in an excruciating heap on the floor. Sweat broke out across his forehead.

Cursing his idiocy, he leaned back against the chair and allowed the shooting pain to subside.

"Well isn't this a charming scene?"

Startled, he looked towards the door. "Henry."

"At your service." His brother made a dramatic bow. He looked like the fugitive he was: completely dishevelled and dirty, with several weeks' worth of beard. Matthias could smell him from where he was.

"Kitty said you wished to see me," he announced in an irreverent voice.

Kitty had also said Henry wanted him dead and here Matthias was, in a most vulnerable position, in a heap on the floor and nothing to hand with which to defend himself.

"I had hoped to find you and help you before Worth did," Matthias said carefully as he tried to inch himself back and lift himself up into the chair.

"Shall I help you?" Henry asked, watching with evident amusement.

"No, thank you." He gave up and remained on the floor.

"I was told you were dead," Henry said bluntly.

"As you can see, I am very much alive," Matthias answered, trying to keep all sarcasm and bitterness from his voice. "Come in and have a drink with me." Matthias held out the decanter to share.

It was the first sign of hesitation that Henry had shown, but he did move forward after a moment and took the matching leather armchair across from Matthias. "I could not be certain you would wish to help me. I assume Kitty told you what I said. That was a charming search party, by the way."

Henry had not totally lost his wits if he realized what was happening. Had his earlier words to Kitty only been said in fear? Matthias waited for Henry to explain.

"I wished to speak with you alone, so I waited. I knew they would come."

"Of course they would. We want to help you."

"Yes, for the family name." Henry's features contorted. "The Matthias I remember would have tossed me to the wolves to let me reap the consequences of my actions."

Matthias could not help but smile a little. "I suppose I can be rather pompous; but I have seen enough death and I certainly do not wish for yours."

"You do not have an heir," he retorted. "Can you still not bring Kitty up to scratch?"

Matthias did not answer that stab. "Why did you do it?"

Anger flashed through Henry's eyes. "I did not mean for him to die. You could not understand."

"I believe you did not kill him on purpose. Often people die from the infection. I was very ill from infection when I arrived back in England. For a month, they did not know if I would live. I meant, rather, why did you gamble?"

"At first it began as a game. I am very, very good at it."

"Then why did you cheat?"

Henry's face turned red. "Because Preston set me up. It was a matter of honour I could not back down from."

"So you wagered a great sum and had to recoup it in one game?"

Henry gave a brief nod of affirmation.

Matthias slowly took a sip of his brandy, wondering how to proceed. "Do you still wish to kill me?"

Henry laughed cynically. "It would certainly solve my problems."

"You would have two murders on your head. Peers cannot commit murder and get away with it, Henry."

"In affairs of honour, they can," he argued.

"Not when you were the one who cheated, and you can hardly call me out and kill me in a duel."

"What would you have me do?"

"Allow us to help you escape."

"But I will never be allowed to come back," he whined.

"One of the consequences of your actions, I am afraid. If you remain it is likely you will hang."

Henry took a glass from the nearby table and filled it from the decanter.

"We have a respectable holding in the West Indies, or you can try your luck somewhere new."

His face wrinkled with distaste. "That place is full of horrid insects and natives."

"Every country has natives." Matthias would dearly love to have him impressed on to a ship or enlisted in the army. He would be rid of his ungrateful, spoiled ideas in less than a fortnight. "I could try to find you a place on a ship," Matthias offered.

"I can barely ride in a carriage, let alone a small craft."

"Then your options are slim. You must leave tonight. Worth was already here, looking for you."

"So soon?"

"Indeed. We have little time. Waverley has his yacht waiting in the cove."

Henry filled a glass with brandy and downed it in one large gulp. "I do not know what to do."

"Almost anywhere would be better than the future you are facing here. You would be Lord of the Manor, so to speak, in Tortola."

"Have you ever been there?"

"No, but Father went there. He had a painting of the plantation house, with beaches and water, in colours of blue and green I have never seen in life. It was quite lovely. There is a sugar plantation and a rum factory. It will not be the society you are used to, of course, but there are quite a number of British living in the vicinity."

"If I do not like it there, what then?"

"You will have to make your own way from there. I can give you a start, but the rest will be up to you."

Henry nodded as though he understood.

"Do you have any belongings to take?"

Henry shook his head. "There was little I could bring with me."

"I have already written a letter to the estate manager at Tortola, in case that was your choice. Along with it is enough money to cover your passage and a good start in the Caribbean. When Hornsby returns, I will have him pack anything of mine you think you might make use of."

Henry swallowed hard. "Thank you, brother."

He stood up and moved in front of where Matthias still sat, propped against the chair. It was not the most civilized position, but it had been a better conversation than Matthias had expected to have. Henry held out a hand to help him up.

"No, Henry! Stop!"

~

"No, Henry!" Kitty screamed when she saw him standing over Matthias, who was on the floor. She leapt on to Henry's back and pulled him away, falling backwards with him on top of her.

"Stop, Kitty!" She heard Matthias's voice. "He is not trying to hurt me."

Having entered in her wake, Waverley and Philip had swiftly moved to subdue Henry, dragging him from his position across her. When they had him standing, with his arms behind his back, everyone stopped and gazed at Matthias, who looked horrified.

"I fell and he was helping me up, that is all."

"Oh, thank God," Kitty said, and let her head fall back on the floor. She had run herself to near exhaustion, but fearing the worst on seeing what had looked like Henry hurting Matthias, she had found a new burst of energy.

Her heart was still thumping in her chest.

"We can let Henry go?" Philip asked. "Because he is in desperate need of a bath. Come to think of it, we probably are as well, now."

Matthias chuckled. "Yes. He could do with a good soaking before he departs."

"You have agreed to go?" Kitty asked hopefully, looking at Henry.

"I do not see any other choice."

"So it will be as planned? My yacht will take him to a port in France and then he will go to Tortola?" the Duke asked.

"Yes. Will someone please send Hornsby to me? I would like him to pack some of my things for Henry and help him be ready."

"He was not long behind us." Philip left to find the batman and Waverley helped Matthias from the floor. Jumping up in an inelegant fashion, Kitty's first order of business was to go and throw her arms around Matthias.

"How did you fall?" she asked Matthias. "For a moment, I thought we were too late."

"That was my fault. When you reached me earlier today, I was at a point of desperation. I had not had a meal in days and was beginning to feel as though the world was closing upon me," Henry explained.

"We should see that you have a proper meal before you go. I will also have Cook pack what she may in the way of provisions."

"Actually," Henry said sheepishly, suddenly looking very like the young boy she had known, "I went to the kitchen first."

Kitty's hands went to her hips. "Do you mean to say you were raiding the larder while we were out looking for you?" she scolded.

"Well, I suppose that is the way of it, but I was starving and I wanted to speak to Matthias alone first, without any interference."

She shook her head. "Be off with you and take a bath and then you will give me a proper hug before you leave."

"Yes, ma'am." He cast an exaggerated bow and then winced.

"Are you hurt?" She could not help but notice the grimace.

"Preston winged me in the hip—fortunately not in a place infection is common, but it still smarts when I move it a certain way."

"I can sympathize," Matthias said wryly. "By the by, where did you hit Preston?"

"In the shoulder, as one is supposed to." Henry shuddered. "I was not trying to kill him, give you my word."

Matthias nodded. "Have that bath now and do us all a favour." Hornsby had arrived and was waiting to go with Henry.

"You are riper than a fly-infested dunghill." Hornsby did not mince words as he wrinkled his nose.

Henry held up his hands in surrender. "I think everyone present has now mentioned the rancid odour of my person." He turned to leave but stopped on the threshold and looked back. "I am happy to see the two of you are together at last, as it should be. Now, brother, I suggest you set about having a proper heir."

When they were finally alone, Matthias sat down on the chair he had earlier vacated and pulled Kitty into his lap.

"Thank you," he said, speaking softly in her ear.

"For what?" She tilted her head back to look up at him.

"For coming to my defence. Henry would not have stood a chance against your wrath." She felt him smile against her forehead. "I do not think my fiercest trooper would have held the line against it either."

"I have always thought they should allow women in the army. War would be a much shorter affair if so. You know what they say about the wrath of a woman scorned. But this..." She choked a little with emotion. "This was pure selfishness."

"How so? You were trying to save my life."

"Because, you tomfool, I do not *ever* want to live without you again." She could feel her chin begin to quiver as the reality of all that had happened—and what could have happened—set in. It felt good to be in his arms at last, but what a journey it had been to get there!

"Ah. If that is the way the wind blows, we had better attend to saying our vows as soon as may be."

"I cannot think Mr. Henderson would object to marrying us later today if he is at liberty to do so. I am sure there has been sufficient time for any objections to be made since Sir Nigel so kindly made the announcement for us at church."

Matthias laughed. "Who would ever have believed we would be thanking him for anything?"

"We must repay him by having a small ceremony at the chapel here and not inviting him."

"You have read my mind," Matthias said and kissed her with such passion that she almost forgot where she was. "Shall we invite the rest of the village instead?"

Kitty laughed. "As amusing as that would be, I think I would prefer a private ceremony amongst those of our friends who are here."

"We can always hold a big celebration afterwards... perhaps when I can walk again."

Some time later, when she was in his arms, leaning snugly against him, Kitty thought she could never be so happy again.

"Do you know why I fell earlier?" Matthias asked.

She shook her head against his shoulder.

"I was trying to walk. That was how Henry found me, actually."

"And he just left you there?"

"No, he offered to help but at that juncture I was not certain he did not mean me harm. I wanted to keep him at a reasonable distance."

"Ah. Should I gather from this that walking did not go very well?"

"I managed one step."

Kitty tried to hide her smile. "That is something, at least. But I do think it best to wait until Dr. Beverly considers you to be ready."

"You are probably correct, my dear, but I wanted to be able to walk you down the aisle at our wedding. I wanted to be whole again for you."

"Oh, Matthias. You need not be anything other than you are. Even if you had lost your leg, it would only be of concern to me because it distressed you."

"I would like to think I would be equally as charitable, were our positions reversed, but if you will have me as I am, I would certainly rather not wait."

"If I will have you...?" she mocked. "I think we have established that you are saddled with me."

"We are saddled with each other," he corrected.

CHAPTER 20

Sounds of people moving about in the entrance hall signalled that it was almost time for Henry to depart.

"It seems our moment of intimacy is over," Matthias said begrudgingly.

"At least there will be many more to come," Kitty reminded him with a quick kiss before she stood up and helped him to his feet.

Hornsby appeared in the doorway and knocked lightly.

"Yes, Hornsby?"

His normally irreverent batman looked uncharacteristically stoic and was turning his hat round and round in his hands.

"Is something amiss?" Matthias was growing worried. "Has Henry changed his mind?"

"No, sir. But if you have no objections, I think I might go with him."

Matthias could not have been more surprised.

"Now that you will have the missus to look after you," he explained with a impudent smirk, "I think Master Henry needs me more than you do. And, if I am being honest," he added with a touch of wistfulness, "the thought of a warm island with soft, balmy breezes sounds more the thing then cold, damp England."

"Why, Hornsby, you sound positively poetic," Matthias teased.

"Would you be amenable to it?" he asked sheepishly.

Matthias exchanged a glance with Kitty and she gave him a nod, a pleased smile lighting her expressive face.

"Actually, Hornsby," he began, "I think it is an excellent idea. I will feel much better about sending Henry there if he has you to look out for him."

Hornsby looked relieved. "Those were my thoughts exactly, Major. I did not want you to think I was abandoning you."

"How could I ever think that? You brought me home and nursed me back to health."

"Well, I had some little help," he said, shuffling his feet back and forth, clearly uncomfortable with the praise.

"Are your belongings packed?"

"Yes, Major."

Matthias heaved himself to his feet and reached for his crutches. Using them, he went over to his batman, propped his crutches against the wall and pulled Hornsby into a strong hug, which ended with them slapping each other on the back.

"Words are not adequate to express my appreciation, my friend. I am glad you will be in Henry's camp. I should have thought of that solution first, but I would not have so presumed on your good nature."

"He is not a bad lad, but he needs someone to keep him in line."

"Quite," Matthias agreed. "I am indebted to you." He held out his hand and shook Hornsby's, then had to turn away before he became a blubbering fool like any raw subaltern leaving home for the first time.

"I must attend to our belongings, sir. I did not pack much. I fancy we won't be needing but half the clothing England requires if it's warm like Spain was."

"Dunford has prepared a packet, which is on my desk. It contains sufficient funds for Henry to make a good start, and letters of introduction to my steward out there."

"Very good, sir."

Henry came downstairs next, accompanied by Waverley and Philip.

"We will see him to the boat in case there should be any trouble from Worth. We will not be leaving your estate and, if necessary, I will remind him of that fact," the Duke remarked.

Matthias knew the Duke was one of the few people Worth would listen to. Nodding, Matthias transferred his gaze to Henry. Clean again and dressed in one of his own coats, his brother had opted to trim his beard rather than shave it off. He was no longer a boy, having been forced to mature overnight. Of a certainty, he was learning his lessons the hard way.

Clearly sensing the two of them needed to talk, Kitty, Waverley and Philip tactfully withdrew from the room.

"I know we have not been as close as we ought, but you are my brother and I wish the best for you," Matthias murmured.

Henry said nothing.

"Will you write to me?"

"I don't understand why you would do this after what I said and did, but thank you," Henry burst out. He held out his hand. Taking it, Matthias pulled his brother forward. He had hugged more today than he might ever have done before in his whole life.

"I do not like goodbyes, so I will be off," Henry said.

"This is not goodbye. We will meet again," Matthias assured him. "Oh, and one piece of advice, if you will?"

Henry looked curious.

"Trust Hornsby. He will be irreverent to the point you might wish to wring his neck, but never a more honest, loyal servant will you find."

"I think that is why I like him so much. You do not mind that he is going with me?" he asked, seemingly with genuine interest.

"I will miss him, but I am glad you will have his valuable experience to call upon."

"I just hope I survive the journey. I am green about the gills merely from thinking about it."

"Larger ships tend to be more steady, I hear. You told Hornsby of your tendency?"

"I did. He said he would get a remedy from Kitty for that."

"It might also include him holding you over the side rail." Matthias laughed. "Fair winds and following seas, brother," he said, offering a little salute.

With Kitty by his side, he watched from the doorway as the men departed.

"That went better than I had hoped," Kitty remarked as the carriage rolled away.

"It will either be the making of him or the death of him," Matthias said thoughtfully.

"If he and Hornsby do not kill one another on the journey," Kitty murmured.

"It will not be easy for Henry. He was not brought up to do anything other than be a gentleman and indulge himself. Even though it is warm there, the climate can take some getting used to. And he will need to humble himself to learn the ways of the people in order to win their respect. I think Hornsby will be a great asset in helping him adjust."

"Then it is a blessing Hornsby thought to accompany him."

"Now he is gone I may admit the fact that, unfortunately, Hornsby will be difficult to replace. However, there are many veterans who will need work. Come inside now, my love. I believe we both need a few hours' rest before we send for Mr. Henderson."

∽

IN THE END, it was the next day before they were able to arrange the wedding. Once everyone had returned from seeing Henry depart, they had fallen into their beds for a well-deserved rest. Sighing as her head touched the pillow, wistfully recalling her love's kisses, Kitty had fallen asleep reflecting that even though she had no wish for a fancy wedding, she still wanted it to be perfect.

Matthias had sent a note to Mr. Henderson, who, when he called the morning following Henry's leave-taking, was easily convinced that the banns had been sufficiently called and was pleased to be called upon to marry them.

The previous afternoon, Kitty, with the help of the Duchess and Lady Amelia, had been able to decorate the drawing room, opening it up into the adjoining conservatory for the occasion.

"I am pleased we were able to be here for the wedding," the Duchess said as they arranged flowers in vases, "although I am sorry events happened as they did with respect to Henry."

Lady Frances squealed with glee. Seated on the floor, she was merrily pulling more petals from a bunch of rose heads than, Kitty suspected, they had in the vases.

"At least he is safe. 'Twould been a different day all together if Worth had caught him," Amelia added. "I did rather expect a wild chase."

"You need not sound so disappointed." Meg shook her head.

"I think he will enjoy having an estate to manage. The Henry I know will find a way to manage," Kitty remarked.

"And now we have something to celebrate," the Duchess said as, tired of her game, little Frances tugged on her mother's gown to be picked up.

Carpets had been rolled up and furniture moved away to be replaced with tables for dining. Vases of roses, in an array of colours from white to yellow to pink, and the scent of the garden filled the room. Kitty could not have been more pleased.

The next morning, Millie helped Kitty dress in one of the beautiful gowns Matthias had ordered from London. It was a simple cream and silver confection which seemed as though it had been made for this occasion. Kitty smiled. "Perhaps it was," she said softly. It was just the type of thing Matthias would have planned for, and it suited her style perfectly.

Millie arranged Kitty's hair in a pile of curls atop her head, weaving a string of pearls through her honeyed caramel locks. Kitty had never felt more like a countess than she did at that moment. Years ago, she had dared to dream of such a thing but that dream had turned to ashes beneath a large, searing flame in the form of the old Earl's tongue. She had learned cruelly the cost of wishing above her station.

Now it felt as though both of them had paid harsh debts of war and widowhood, and she hoped they would find happiness at last.

A knock on the door announced the arrival of the Duke and Duchess, come to escort her to the chapel.

"You look beautiful, Kitty," Meg said.

The Duke held out a small box to her. "Matthias asked me to give these to you."

Kitty accepted the small, ornately paper mâchéd box painted with intricate little flowers and birds and opened it.

"These belonged to his mother," she said as she took the string of pearls and matching earrings.

"He said she would have wanted you to have them."

Kitty nodded tearfully, knowing how pleased the Countess would have been to see this day happen. The Earl, on the other hand, was no doubt rolling over in his grave. He had not been a horrible man, just a prideful aristocrat. It was not as if Kitty had been born a guttersnipe. She had been related to the Countess which he had seemed to forget. That was all past now and Kitty for one knew she would appreciate her position more for what she'd been through. Certainly, she would never take Matthias or her home for granted.

"I found this in my things. I had meant to give it to you before, but this seems like a perfect occasion," the Duke said and he held out Peter's old satchel, which she thought had been lost.

In it were his favourite things—his hunting crop, a silver flask which matched one Matthias had, his worn leather journal, and inside a smaller pouch were his old pocket watch and small, golden band she'd given him in that other wedding day so long ago. Today was utterly different.

"Thank you." There was little else to say, but perhaps having his things would help bring closure.

The chapel was a short walk from the house. It was a small structure of golden stone, matching the house, with Gothic arches and vibrant stained glass windows. The towered steeple attached to the church was almost as large as the chapel itself.

When they entered the nave and Kitty saw Matthias standing before the altar, waiting for her, she felt humbled and grateful, as though her life had merely been a journey to this moment. He had donned his regimentals for the occasion, still presenting an impressive figure despite his infirmity. The way he looked at her near stole her breath away. She felt like a sweetmeat ready to be devoured.

Then he smiled at her—in a way that made her feel she was the most important thing in the world to him. The Duke handed her to Matthias when they reached the altar and stepped back. Taking her hand in his, Matthias squeezed it warmly.

"Finally," he said, loud enough that the few guests could hear.

Kitty turned when she heard a familiar laugh. "James!" she exclaimed, smiling brightly at him. Her attention being wholly upon Matthias during her sedate promenade down the aisle, she had not noticed their friend.

"He arrived just in time," Matthias whispered.

The Rector cleared his throat. "Shall we begin?" Lifting his voice a little to be heard by the congregation, he continued, "May I say we have waited a long time for this day. I know you loved Master Peter, and I know he is here with us this day in spirit, giving his blessing."

Kitty had sworn she would not cry, but tears filled her eyes and threatened to spill down her cheeks. She looked upward and gave a little nod, truly feeling that Peter's spirit was with them.

"I feel him too," Matthias said quietly.

Throughout the ceremony, as they said their vows, took holy communion and signed the register, Kitty cherished every moment. She was filled with a deep happiness that could only come from an inner peace she had not known before.

When they left the chapel, little Lady Frances threw rose petals at them from the height of her daddy's arms. She giggled with infectious delight.

"I think you may have something there, my lady," Matthias said to the little cherub and kissed her cheek.

"Wa?" she asked, pointing in the direction of the lake.

"You wish to go on the swing again? Perhaps later, my dear," Matthias said with a chuckle.

They walked in a group back to the house, where Cook had prepared a veritable feast. Game hens, cutlets of veal and joints of lamb were offered with rich sauces, along with various vegetable dishes including asparagus wrapped in bacon, carrots glazed with maple syrup and potatoes roasted in butter and herbs. Fresh rolls wafted their tempting scent alongside them was set a dish of yellow butter, a chocolate cream, a plate of lemon meringues, and a beautiful sponge cake soaked with a toffee glaze.

There was no dancing, out of respect for Matthias's injury, and they therefore sat around a table, mostly being entertained by James relating stories of his visit to Scotland.

"I cannot tell you how relieved I was to receive your letter," James declared after Waverley and Philip had made their toasts. "I desperately needed an excuse to leave which my mother would believe."

Everyone laughed as James had a tendency to say most things in a way that evoked humour.

"Is your mother inclined to be overbearing?" Amelia asked with sympathy.

"Only in the manner of trying to hoist on to me the marriageable daughters of the clan McKiernan." He shuttered dramatically.

"What is wrong with them?"

"Nothing at all if you have a fancy for ladies to resemble a cross between an Arabian and a Clydesdale. although, come to think of it, that might be an insult to the Clydesdale."

Sitting beside Kitty, Matthias almost choked on his champagne.

"Then how did you manage to escape?" Amelia prodded.

"I might have exaggerated who would be in attendance here." He made a sheepish gesture.

"I must say, James, now that the rest of us are married, perhaps you should take a wife," Waverley said pompously.

"Why ever would that compel me to do so? No offence intended, ladies," he replied, flashing his charming smile at each of them in turn.

"None taken," the Duchess said with a languid wave of her hand.

"My lifestyle is hardly conducive to a family," he added.

"You mean to return to the army?" Waverley asked.

"There is little else for me. I have nothing to offer any lady in her right mind. My parents are holding on to an ideal that no longer exists. They see heritage and charm in a draughty stone house with no plumbing. The fields are fallow or barren, and most of the tenants were wise enough to move to America."

"Do not underrate yourself, James. Any lady would be lucky to have you," Amelia said. "Just wear your most dashing uniform and tell them of your heroic rescues of maidens in distress."

"You could always marry an heiress," Philip suggested, then winked at his wife.

"There is always the option of your housekeeper," Kitty said impishly.

Matthias groaned.

"Why do I feel as though I am missing a delicious piece of a story?" James asked.

"Because you are. When Matthias arrived back from the Continent, Kitty was acting as his housekeeper," the Duke explained.

"Tut, tut," James scolded. "That is an old trick, Kitty."

Kitty narrowed her gaze at him.

"Do you remember Nasty Nigel?" Waverley asked, looking as if he had swallowed a sour lemon.

James wrinkled his face with distaste. "How could I forget?"

"It was he who brought them together."

"It was he who forced the issue," Matthias corrected.

"I can see your indebtedness to him is overflowing." James made a dramatic show of looking around at the guests. "I would have turned around and left if he had been here."

Once the laughter had died down, Matthias slowly pushed back in his chair and stood up; everyone quieted, sensing the mood had changed.

"I should like to make one last toast." Matthias held up his glass. "To Peter," he began, then was forced to pause as emotion choked him. When he had composed himself, he started again. "To Peter, who, even though he had the audacity to leave us behind, showed all of us the meaning of honour."

"To Peter." They charged their glasses. "*Pietas et honos.*"

AFTERWORD

Author's note: British spellings and grammar have been used in an effort to reflect what would have been done in the time period in which the novels are set. While I realize all words may not be exact, I hope you can appreciate the differences and effort made to be historically accurate while attempting to retain readability for the modern audience.

Thank you for reading *The Ones Left Behind.* I hope you enjoyed it. If you did, please help other readers find this book:

1. This ebook is lendable, so send it to a friend who you think might like it so she or he can discover me, too.
2. Help other people find this book by writing a review.
3. Sign up for my new releases at www.Elizabethjohnsauthor.com, so you can find out about the next book as soon as it's available.
4. Connect with me at any of these places:

www.Elizabethjohnsauthor.com
Facebook

Instagram
Bookbub
Goodreads
elizabethjohnsauthor@gmail.com

ACKNOWLEDGMENTS

There are many, many people who have contributed to making my books possible.

My family, who deals with the idiosyncrasies of a writer's life that do not fit into a 9 to 5 work day.

Dad, who reads every single version before and after anyone else— that alone qualifies him for sainthood.

Wilette and Anj, who take my visions and interpret them, making them into works of art people open in the first place.

My team of friends who care about my stories enough to help me shape them before everyone else sees them.

Heather who helps me say what I mean to!

And to the readers who make all of this possible.
I am forever grateful to you all.

ALSO BY ELIZABETH JOHNS

Surrender the Past

Seasons of Change

Seeking Redemption

Shadows of Doubt

Second Dance

Through the Fire

Melting the Ice

With the Wind

Out of the Darkness

After the Rain

Ray of Light

Moon and Stars

First Impressions

The Governess

On My Honour

Not Forgotten

An Officer Not a Gentleman

Made in the USA
Las Vegas, NV
10 February 2022

43641375R00122